Big O Romeo

(book seven of the Royal Romeos series)
by Jenny Gardiner

What people are saying about Jenny Gardiner's books:

"A fun, sassy read! A cross between Erma Bombeck and Candace Bushnell, reading Jenny Gardiner is like sinking your teeth into a chocolate cupcake…you just want more."

--Meg Cabot, NY Times bestselling author of Princess Diaries, Queen of Babble and more, on Sleeping with Ward Cleaver

"With a strong yet delightfully vulnerable voice, food critic Abbie Jennings embarks on a soulful journey where her love for banana cream pie and disdain for ill-fitting Spanx clash in hilarious and heartbreaking ways. As her body balloons and her personal life crumbles, Abbie must face the pain and secret fears she's held inside for far too long. I cheered for her the entire way."

--Beth Hoffman, NY Times bestselling author of *Saving CeeCee Honeycutt* on *Slim to None*

"Jenny Gardiner has done it again--this fun, fast-paced book is a great summer read."

--Sarah Pekkanen, NY Times bestselling author of *The Opposite of Me*, on *Slim to None*

"As Sweet as a song and sharp as a beak, *Bite Me* really soars as a memoir about family--children and husbands, feathers and fur--and our capacity to keep loving though life may occasionally bite."

--Wade Rouse, bestselling author of At Least in the City Someone Would Hear Me Scream

Chapter One

IF there was one thing Francesco Romeo hated more than having to attend a party full of strangers, it was having to attend a costume party full of strangers dressed in stupid outfits. So it was with great reluctance that he agreed to go to the seventieth birthday party of his mother's best friend, Elettra Giovanetti, who'd decreed that their little corner of Tuscany hadn't had a decent costume party in what seemed like centuries. In Francesco's humble opinion, it hadn't been long enough. Because to him, there was no such thing as a decent costume party.

For one thing, people tended to dress like fools at those events. Men usually looked like complete imbeciles, and women often felt the need to indulge in their inner beer wench, which, okay, sometimes wasn't such a bad thing—at least from a visual perspective—but seriously, it was downright odd when women took on the persona of the outfit they had on.

He still remembered the last such party he'd attended, when a voluptuous woman who had been his teacher in primary school donned a cleavage-revealing corset top, wedged a cup of maraschino cherries between her generous bosom, and insisted that guests pop her cherry all night long. You simply couldn't unsee that shit. Particularly when it belonged to the woman who taught you the alphabet, phonics, and how to get along with others.

Also, it's weird, standing there talking to your hairdresser, who's pretending to be Dorothy from *The Wizard of Oz*, when all along you know she's just Maria Valdetti with the distinctive mole on the tip of her nose, who's been styling your hair since you were about fourteen years old. The whole thing seemed sadly regressive to him.

Nevertheless he found himself at the party rental shop minutes before closing time, waiting in line for a Three Musketeers costume at the behest of his mother, who he hated to displease. It didn't matter that there weren't two other musketeers to complete the theme. Neither his brothers nor friends would agree to wear hats with feathers—they were for sissies, they claimed—plus all the normal costumes were rented by the time Francesco finally sucked it up and went in search of something to wear to this miserable party.

He was seriously regretting not snatching up the Darth Vader costume before it was nabbed by a wiser partygoer. At the time, he figured it would impede his chances to make out with a woman, what with his entire face covered by a mask. In hindsight, perhaps that would have been a better alternative.

His remaining choices were to go as a seventeenth-century French swashbuckler or settle for the oversized, body-odor-drenched Barney the Purple Dinosaur costume, which he was certain hadn't been cleaned or worn in about twenty years. At least he had a chance of getting laid in his chosen costume. Though between the girlie stockings, thigh-high leather boots, and, yeah, that gargantuan damned feather that kept obscuring his vision, he wasn't banking on much action from anyone under the age of 300.

He'd waited till, quite literally, the last possible minute to grab his threads, which meant he'd have to change clothes at the shop. That probably wasn't such a bad thing, since it spared him the ridicule at home. Though naturally, his brothers would double down on it once they found him at the party. He hoped that in the thick of the crowd, they'd miss finding him. Besides, he was going to be cloaked in so much frippery, maybe he'd go unnoticed altogether. A man could only hope.

Allie Ledbetter was nervous about this party. New to the area and not all that fluent in Italian, she wasn't sure if it was a good or bad thing to be virtually invisible at the costume party she was invited to attend in honor of the mother of her new boss, winemaker Giovanni Giovanetti. Apparently he was throwing the fête for her seventieth birthday. It seemed a little weird showing up at a stranger's party for such an auspicious occasion. But, oh well. In her line of work, she had become accustomed to integrating into whatever environment she found herself in temporarily, even if it meant showing up at some granny's birthday shindig.

Besides, Allie loved a good costume party; it was fun to see how creative people could get for them. In fact back home, she'd dressed in many elaborate getups for Halloween parties over the years, once even donning a multilayered, hoop-skirted Marie Antoinette costume, complete with a huge headache-inducing wig. But far from home and minus her trusty sewing machine, she was going to have to make do with a more rudimentary outfit—one that always seemed to work for last-minute events.

On a day trip to Rome, she'd found some perfect crushed black velvet at Fratelli Bassetti Tessuti, a renowned fabric shop favored by the country's fashion cognoscenti. Simply wandering the store alone, reveling in the breathtaking fabrics, was worth the trip to the city. While there, she picked up some sewing notions including a packet of needles, straight pins, black thread, and fabric scissors, and even found some fiberfill. Back in Tuscany, she sat on the terrace of the plush guest cottage at Giovanetti Vineyards, sipping a crisp Italian rosata wine from that same vineyard as the intense summer sun hung low in the sky. She was having a thoroughly lovely time hand stitching and stuffing her cat tail and securing kitty-cat ears onto a headband as well. Her costume came together with a black satin camisole top and a pair of black skinny jeans. With her long, wavy, streaky blond hair and hazel eyes, she'd make a perfectly acceptable feline for the night.

When the time came to dress for the party, Allie drew thick, black Cleopatra-style eyeliner along the edge of her lids, slicked on some extra layers of mascara, and wrapped her tresses along the fat wand of her curling iron to create cascading curls. She debated going all in with whiskers and decided it was necessary to complete the transformation, so she traced slender whisker lines along her cheeks, then finished the look by coloring the tip of her nose black with an eyebrow pencil.

She pinned the tail to her jeans and tugged them on,

then slipped on the delicate cami top. Standing sideways, she assessed herself in the full-length mirror, pressed her hands along her thighs to straighten out her jeans, and nodded.

"Not too bad," she said as she reached for a pair of strappy black sandals to complete the look. She slid on the headband ears and slipped out the door of the cottage.

She walked along a slate pathway to the main house, a sprawling pale pink two-story stucco palazzo like the many that peppered the hillsides in this part of Tuscany. Expensive cars lined the driveway, and a throng of guests in imaginative outfits paraded through the rose garden as they made their way to the dramatic front entryway of the Giovanetti home.

She'd only been in Tuscany for a few days, but so far, what she'd seen sure made her want to stay. Between the rolling hillsides clad in patchworked fields with rows of vines soon to be heavy with fruit, and those cloaked with the gnarled branches of ancient olive trees, this land felt magical. Throw in magnificent manor homes that had witnessed history over many hundreds of years and the late-day color of light—a breathtaking combination of damask rose and ripe melon—and, well, there was something about this place that spoke to her.

She entered through the massive oak doors that were drawn open on this temperate summer evening and was handed a flute of top-tier Italian prosecco and escorted by a waiter dressed like one of Cinderella's footmen to a wide, dramatic, harlequin-tiled terrace along the back of the palazzo that overlooked the valley below. High above, a flock of birds darted to and fro. She felt a momentary pang of anxiety, knowing that in a matter of days it was going to

be her job—well, hers and Lola's, her trusty peregrine falcon—to ensure massive flocks of grape-loving starlings stayed clear of her bosses' harvest. It's what she'd been doing for a couple of years now, first in California, and now in Italy, letting Lola and other birds of prey loose to intimidate the population of birds that constantly vexed the growers of wine grapes.

Lola had become well-known after Allie gave a series of lectures about this at several winegrowers' conventions. Giovanni had reached out to her shortly thereafter, hoping to bring her to Tuscany to minimize the frustrating and, at times, astronomical loss of grapes leading up to his grape harvest, thanks to greedy starlings. Thoughts of Lola would wait until morning. Tonight she was given a free pass not to worry about her charge and to enjoy herself instead.

She marveled at the creativity of some of the costumes people wore. One woman dressed as Little Red Riding Hood clutched a leash attached to a gorgeous white-and-gray husky dog with bright blue eyes wearing a sleeping cap and purple pajamas: the Big Bad Wolf doing business as Grandma. Very clever.

A man moseyed by dressed as a stick figure, wearing an all-white outfit on which the black stick shape had been painted. One couple had donned an ocean theme: the woman was costumed as a mermaid and the man, a fierce Father Neptune. Another person was dressed as an octopus. There was a hula dancer and a Barbie look-alike and several zombies, though she couldn't help but think it wouldn't be much fun to get up close and personal with a man oozing faux bodily fluids. Yep, zombie was not the costume to wear if you went to the party in search of a love interest.

Not that she was on the prowl or anything: for one thing, she wasn't going to be staying here for long. Once the grapes were harvested, she would move on to another gig, far from Italy. Plus, after her last fiasco of a relationship, in which her fiancé Ben decided it made sense to let her know only weeks before the wedding that he preferred men, she was a little gun-shy about guys. Tonight, she was going to wear her costume, enjoy some drinks, perhaps make some small talk if anyone spoke enough English to conduct a conversation with her, and call it a night.

Or so she thought.

"Meow." She heard a deep, resonant voice purr behind her. She turned to see perhaps the most handsome man she'd ever laid eyes on, with sooty, soulful brown eyes and wavy, rich, peat-colored hair that pretty much begged her fingers to run through it. He was dressed as one of the Three Musketeers, which happened to top Allie's fantasy of the type of man she'd love to be taken by. It fit with her love of falconry and her passion for the romance of the adventurous days of swashbuckling men clinking swords and defending fair maidens.

Damn. This particular musketeer could defend her honor any old day.

She let out a purr of contentment.

So much for avoiding men for a while.

Chapter Two

FRANCESCO decided he had to dial down his disdain for costume parties. Sure the woman standing by the bar dressed as Elvira, Mistress of the Night did not appeal to him. Despite her voluminous breasts, which were more than peeking out of the V in her dress that went all the way to her navel, there was something to be said for leaving a bit to the imagination. Sometimes more wasn't always better.

And the buxom woman dressed as a milkmaid who asked if he wanted to squeeze her teats was a little too obvious. Maybe if he was feeling super desperate... but no. Not even then. And he was a breast man!

But then he laid eyes on the kitty cat standing alone against the limestone balustrade on the terrace, and he decided he needed to reevaluate his blanket revulsion of this particular party genre. Because wow, meow, that one instantly took his breath away. He'd love to stroke that kitty cat in more ways than one.

And that tail alone... Though his curiosity was certainly piqued by the velvety one dangling from her butt, what he meant was that ass, perfectly shaped in a pair of tight jeans that hugged those two round globes, one of his many favorite parts of a woman. As an added bonus, her legs went on and on, ending in some sexy little high-heeled sandals, complete with vampy black polish on her toes. His eyes scanned up her body and stopped at nipples that were poking out from her silky top, leaving him curious—make that desperate—to see even more. On second thought, sometimes more could be a good thing.

As his gaze continued upward, he was pleased with her face: bowed lips in an innocent smile and wide, kind, earthy-golden eyes that fit her cat costume perfectly, topped by coils of shiny, blond waves he'd love to grab on to while she… Ugh. He had to tamp down that thought or he'd scare the poor kitty away.

Meow indeed.

He had nothing to lose—after all, he was dressed like a damned musketeer—so he snuck up behind her and purred into her ear.

She turned around and stared. He wasn't sure if it was the crazy getup he was wearing or what prevented her from saying a word, and it made him nervous to think he looked like a giant wanker and she was devising how many different ways to tell him to beat it.

But she then lifted a brow and smiled. "Well, hi there, stranger." She made a point of looking him up and down. "I've gotta say—I do love a man in tights."

And Francesco breathed a sigh of relief because there were likely far more women turned off by that than on.

"Then that makes us even because I love a beautiful pussy when I see one."

She laughed. "I'm not sure whether to laugh or be shocked at your impertinence." She pretended to fan her face.

"Impertinence? Me?" he batted his eyelashes in jest.

"I was trying to use a word that a damsel in distress in the time of the musketeers might use."

"Are you in the habit of mining the language of antiquity?"

She shook her head. "Nah, but I've read plenty of historical romance novels."

Francesco cocked his head. "You mean bodice rippers?"

She scrunched her nose. "No one uses that term anymore. Besides, I don't opt to read novels where rogue men force themselves on women."

"What do these rogue men do, then?"

She laughed. "Sorry, this is sort of a weird conversation. I guess I'd say they seduce their way in. Much kinder and gentler that way."

"So it's the seduction that appeals to you."

The woman lifted a curious brow. "Doesn't that appeal to pretty much everyone?"

He held his hands up. "You'll find no argument from me. I'm a big fan of the seduction."

She sized him up again. "With an outfit like that, you'll hardly have to lift a finger."

"Ahhh, then all I need to do is boast about the size of my, um, peacock feather to win the hand of a fair maiden?" He flicked at the thing hanging over his eyes and smiled broadly.

She blurted out a laugh. "Well, I for one always love a man with a big, uh, feather." She pulled her hand away, then fingered the large one dangling in front of his face. "Though I suspect this is an ostrich feather and has absolutely nothing to do with a cock, 'pea' or larger."

Francesco's interest was indeed piqued. This woman

was surprisingly comfortable making suggestive conversation with the likes of him. How could he not want to see where this led?

He held out his hand. "Francesco Romeo," he said, reaching for hers.

The kitty cat extended her hand and he gently pulled it toward his lips and pressed them to the back of her fingers. She blushed, which he loved, as it showed him that while she was not afraid to get sassy with him, she also had some moral constraints that probably gave her great internal conflict. Clearly it wasn't the norm for her to talk to a man like this. Maybe it was the costume—perhaps it let her hide behind it to reveal a more unencumbered version of herself? He'd take this over the cherry-popping beer wench any day.

"I'm Allie. Allie Ledbetter."

"Enchanted. Or as we say in Italy, *incantato*."

"Ooohhh… Incantato…" she played with the word on her tongue, which made him want to reach out with his own tongue and tangle their words together. "In France, it would be *enchanté*. *N'est-ce pas?*"

"You speak French?"

She shrugged and held up her hand with a small space between thumb and forefinger. "*Un peu*. A little bit."

"Parlo Italiano?"

She shook her head. "I've tried to learn a little with the Duo Lingo app, but I'd embarrass myself if I attempted to communicate with it. By all means, though, please do use your mother tongue. It makes me swoon a bit to listen to spoken Italian."

Francesco rubbed his hands together. "So I've got three things in my favor: I'm dressed like a swashbuckling man of yore, which turns you on. I speak Italian, which makes you swoon. And of course, there's that big, uh, feather of mine. What more do I need to convince you of my worth and honor?"

"Yikes." She wagged her finger. "I suppose I showed my hand too soon. Remind me next time to keep my big mouth shut."

"*A il contrario.*" He rubbed his stubbled chin with his thumb and forefinger. "To the contrary. For me, it's quite a turn-on when a woman owns her sexuality."

She blushed again. Even the pale skin on her chest turned rosy. He wondered if the soft flesh underneath the edge of her shirt had also shaded pink. He imagined slipping his fingers beneath the top of the silky black fabric and his mouth grew dry. It had been too long since he'd been laid.

"Speaking of size," she said, reaching for the cutlass secured to his waistband, "I like your saber."

"Why, thank you. And it's sized to your satisfaction?" He knew he might be pushing the envelope with his double entendres, but he decided to go for broke.

"The bigger the better." She licked her lips. "But I wonder—"

Francesco couldn't wait to hear what she wondered. He hoped it had something to do with the many uses of that oversized épée of his.

"Why do musketeers carry swords? Aren't they supposed to be all about the musket they're named after?"

So much for a suggestive innuendo. But he had a rebound response to get back on track. "Because swords are far sexier."

"Oh really?" she crossed her arms over her chest.

"How so?"

"You can use your imagination." He drew his sword. "Imagine where that sword might penetrate." He lifted the saber and gently drew it beneath her breasts like a threatening Barbary Coast pirate might. "Isn't this how they do it? Here," he said, moving the small, rounded tip and pressing it toward her pubic bone. "Or here?"

"Hmmm," she said. "I would think if you were looking for penetration with something that size you'd have some other more appealing options."

As his eyes grew wide, they were interrupted by a drunk man dressed as a monkey asking where the bar was.

Francesco turned to Allie and reached his arm out to link with hers. "What say we tuck into a more private corner where we could at least monkey around without being interrupted by strange simians?" He offered his arm for her to thread hers through.

They walked toward the farthest end of the terrace, far from the crowd, where there were no lights and they could have some privacy.

"You're not quite like any woman I've met before," he said.

She shrugged. "I'm just plain old me."

He shook his head. "Trust me, there is nothing plain about you. I know a gorgeous pussy when I see one."

She blushed again and playfully smacked her hand to his chest. "Stop. You're embarrassing me."

"Mea culpa," he said. "I don't want to make you feel uncomfortable." He pointed to the far corner of the stone railing then crooked his finger for her to follow him. "I have something I want to show you."

He steered her up against the railing, pointing far off

to the right. "Can you see it?"

She turned her head in the direction he was motioning. "What?"

"There," he said, nodding in that direction. "The full moon is beginning to rise on the horizon. You can barely see an orange sliver as it creeps skyward."

"Ahhh," she said. "It's beautiful."

"It's known as the thunder moon," he said. "Because of the propensity for volatile storms at this time of year."

"Sounds tempestuous."

"Lively and heated. Exactly the way I like it." Francesco came up behind Allie and leaned his body against her back, bringing his arms around her, tucking his thumbs into the front pockets of her jeans. As he pressed along that sweet kitty-cat tail of hers, he grew harder.

"I thought you'd sheathed that saber of yours." She turned and gave him a sly look with a wink.

He leaned down and nibbled on the edge of her ear as he whispered into it. "Sometimes it doesn't want to be so confined."

Allie pressed her ass up against him and he moaned. His mouth trailed along her ear, delivering tiny kisses and bites, then along her jawline until his mouth found hers and he paused, pressing his lips to hers. She turned her head slightly and opened her mouth to him, allowing him to slick his tongue along the edge of her teeth as he sought out her tongue. With a moan, she slid her tongue along his, deepening the kiss.

Francesco slid his hands along Allie's hips, moving up toward her breasts, where he cupped his hands over each one and rubbed them. She reached behind to press his body toward her even more, which thrust her breasts toward his reach. He took that as a sign and moved his fingers along the top edge of her camisole, sliding his fingers down, nudging her barely there strapless bra out of the way as his fingers sought those hard nipples he'd desperately wanted to touch earlier. He pressed them between his thumb and forefinger, massaging them as they grew tighter with his ministrations. She gasped. Good Lord, if he wasn't careful he was going to lose it right here on the terrace of his mother's best friend's palazzo, which would not be cool. He broke the kiss but continued to play with her nipples and massage her breasts.

"How about we slip away from here and maybe go catting around the neighborhood for a while. If you're lucky, maybe I'll even howl at the moon like a good tomcat." Francesco practically hummed the words in her ear.

Allie bit her lip, then shook her head. "I'm sorry. I'm afraid this is all happening so fast," she said. "I mean on the one hand, yeesh. I've never made out with a musketeer before, and I'd love to keep playing. On the other hand, we've barely introduced ourselves to one another. It's probably a good idea to put the brakes on this for the time being."

Francesco's lip thrust out in a pout. "But we were having so much fun." He shifted around and they were now face-to-face.

Allie squinted. "I know. I'm sorry. I let myself get carried away. It must have been the costume. I let my guard down. I've got to focus on my work. I can't allow distractions like this to get in the way."

"Distraction?" He frowned. "Here I thought we had a mutual attraction."

She shrugged. "Attraction. Distraction. I don't know. But I need to run. It was fun, though."

With that, she turned and ran off toward the exit, not even turning to say goodbye.

"But I didn't even get your number," Francesco said, holding up his fingers as if to flag her down. Alas, she was too far away to hear him. He scrubbed his hand over his face and looked down to his palm, which was smeared with black makeup that had transferred from the kitty cat's face to his: all that was left of the best time he'd had in a long time.

Dammit, he hated costume parties.

Chapter Three

WELL. That didn't go according to plan.

What the hell was she thinking, going at it like a cat in heat with that man out of the complete ever-loving blue? Correction: that *musketeer*. Of course. That was her problem. Dressed like the intrepid swashbuckler, he was her fantasy come to life: the one who would swing down from the rigging of a tall ship to save her from the devilish pirate who'd threatened her chastity.

She laughed. Chastity. As if. Hell, she'd chucked that out the window with the disappointing Eric Sternholtz in, what, eleventh grade? And she'd kind of regretted it the minute the deed was done. At the time, well, he was cute, and he was a great kisser, but that was where his seductive talents ceased. When it came to sexual intercourse, he was the Peter Principle in action.

The whole virginity thing seemed like such a damned nuisance—after all, who decided to put such a bounty on being the first one to blaze that ridiculous trail anyhow? Men. Men were simply too weird. It was like some sexual version of peeing on yet another fire hydrant.

She was over that whole nonsense long ago, along with the patriarchy that accompanied it, and was more than happy to cash in her V-card and be done with it. Thus she gladly gave it up to some guy she hardly cared about but who looked good in his tennis whites (he played on the school team).

The only reason she regretted it was that it was so disappointing; wham, bam, thank you, ma'am would have been an upgrade. Technically she wasn't even certain he'd gotten that little thing of his all the way in before he managed to get himself off. He seemed embarrassed by that, and afterward, there wasn't much conversation and certainly no cuddling—the deed was done, after all, in the middle bench of his parents' ancient Dodge Caravan that reeked of wet dog—hardly the most romantic of settings. She remembered at one point looking down at the floor of the van and seeing petrified fast food french fries, and it seemed metaphoric in some way.

Over the years, she'd certainly had her share of unremarkable intimate encounters with entirely forgettable men, but so far, nothing that stood out in her mind in a particularly good way. Maybe she'd been going after the wrong type of guy. Well, according to her best friend Harper Landry, she did exactly that: always the self-absorbed ones, the pretty boys, the ones all the girls made a fuss over. And Harper was right. Rarely were those types the ones who put out much for the woman. They weren't looking for reciprocity; rather they wanted continued affirmation about how great they were. Yawn. That bored her.

Maybe that's why she figured what the hell, why not enjoy a little playtime with a tall, dark stranger while she was in an unfamiliar land and knew no one. It had a "Mark of Zorro" feel to it. At least that was what she was telling herself as she scurried back to her cottage, embarrassed that she practically let the man rub one out on her in public.

"Thank goodness you'll never see him again," she said aloud as she shut the door and pressed her body against it as if keeping out any uninvited musketeers. "Next time, you'll use some discretion and if you're going to do that, at least do it when there aren't a hundred pairs of eyes potentially on you."

She walked through the hallway and caught sight of herself in a wall mirror. Her kitty-cat nose was smeared, which meant her musketeer—Francesco—was that his name?—likely bore the telltale signs of their little tête-à-tête as well. She laughed, wondering if people had asked why he had black makeup smeared across his face. But then she wondered if by now, he'd instead picked up where they left off with some other costumed woman, one who didn't pull an abrupt about-face right when things were getting interesting: a classic cock-tease. She could hardly blame him if he did. Dammit. Maybe she should have gone for it. What was the harm?

The harm was you didn't even know the man! She closed her eyes and shook her head, annoyed at her impulsivity.

Allie plunked down on the sofa and turned on the television, only to realize that all of the programs on TV were ridiculous game shows involving a lot of practically naked women. Italian television at its finest. Which only made her realize if she hadn't reined in her libido, that would likely be her current state: with a man dressed as a swashbuckler. Dammit. Maybe she should've gone with her gut.

She decided to call Harper for reassurance. She would be home from work by now, and she was always good at talking her off the ledge.

Harper answered after the third ring.

"What up, homey girl?" she said.

Allie could hear lots of noise in the background. "Where are you? It sounds like a party."

"I wish," Harper said. "Sadly I'm on a blind date that almost makes me wish I was blind—I mean it's not that the guy is ugly, it's that, well on top of being a complete jerk, he's ugly."

"Oh, sweetie, I'm sorry," Allie said. "I hate to ask who set you up."

"The organist at church is a friend of my mom's. She said her nephew was a lovely young man. Young being a relative term, because I think he's approaching fifty. And has a bad whiskey nose, which was no doubt made worse by the three consecutive drinks he's thrown down since I got here."

"Charming."

"He's one of those guys who spits when he talks and I keep having to wipe my face discreetly. The worst thing is that nothing he says is worth the effort it takes me to clear his saliva from my flesh, because he seems to only want to say mean things about people, including his aunt. So thank God you called and I could slip away."

"You might want to consider not returning to your seat," Allie said.

"Believe me, I'm tempted to disappear. But I don't want to be rude or it'll get back to his aunt and my mom will pitch a fit. Instead, I'll use your call as an excuse to leave—I'll tell him it's a family emergency." She paused. "So, what's your emergency?"

Allie laughed. "In which case you'll be glad I

interrupted your hot date to tell you how I interrupted my own hot date. Well, it wasn't a date. But it was turning into one rapidly. Actually, not at all a date. More like a one-night stand. Hell, it probably would have been more like a one-hour stand. Or a five-minute stand if I'd have let his hands roam any further."

"I'm sorry, but you are not making a bit of sense. What the hell are you talking about? And feel free to take an inordinately long time explaining because it spares me from having to return to my seat across from that dismal date." She giggled.

Allie let out a deep sigh. "I mean, you know me. You know my bad luck with men. What did you call Jonathan Rotor, that guy who I dated awhile back?"

"Jonathan Rover. Because he was such a dirty dog."

"Yeah. That. I was so oblivious that he had a second date with someone else the same night he and I had our last date. That was good you saw through him."

"Sweetie, I've got your back. Especially when you're too clueless to see the obvious."

"Yeah, yeah. I know. It's why I've avoided relationships since him. But I don't know. I guess the idea of being with a guy is no longer a nonstarter. So then I went to this costume party tonight. And I was kind of bored and a little bit lonely and this guy came up behind me and whispered in my ear and when I turned around he was dressed like a musketeer and—"

"I have a feeling I know where this is going."

"Because you know about my little fetish with that whole thing."

"Yup. I know. The hat—with the feather. The square jaw. The strong musculature. That cape. Those thigh-high boots—"

"Seriously. The boots. I had boot envy with the ones he had on. Dark brown leather, cuffed at the top. They were hot."

"So, this guy whispers in your ear and what, you pull down your pants and do it in the ballroom?"

"Stop! It wasn't like that."

"Elaborate, please."

"Well we got to talking, and the conversation kept being full of double entendres. And did I mention he looked crazy hot? I mean picture the sexiest Italian man, right? Tall, with that shiny, wavy dark hair. His eyes, they were like windows to his soul."

"This sounds like a line in one of those historical romance novels you read."

"But I'm serious. There was something about him that spoke to me."

"It suggested you do him?"

"I didn't do him!"

"Well, then why are you calling me, all up in arms?"

"Because I didn't do him!"

"Wait, so the man of your dreams—or should I say fantasies—shows up, talks dirty to you, you do a little awkward grope and pinch, then you don't go home with him. Only now you're upset that you didn't go home with him. Do I have that right?"

Allie sighed again. "Yes. Okay? I could have slept with him. I mean things were moving fast and they were moving in that direction. But we were at a party, with lots of people around, and then next thing you know his hands are all over me and—*Gah!* I didn't know what to do. I mean it felt right—how could it not have? But it felt wrong, if that makes sense."

"And given the chance of following your heart or your head, you followed your head."

"It was a little premature to follow my heart, don't you think? I'd barely met the man. He was a tall, dark, mysterious stranger."

"But he was super hot."

"Yeah, but I didn't even know him."

"So, what happened? Maybe you should have just said you wanted to go on a date."

"I kind of freaked out. One minute he's got his hands down my shirt, the next minute I'm running off like Cinderella worrying that the clock is about to strike midnight."

"So you were going at it—in public, at a party—and then you chickened out and ran away?"

Allie shrugged, not that her friend could see that. "Womp. Yep. I weenied out. I probably missed out on the best sex of my life."

"You can always reach out to him and go for round two."

She shook her head. "Except that I don't know how to get ahold of him. All I know is his name is Francesco something. Romeo, maybe?"

"Ooooh, Romeo. Sounds sexy. Why don't you Google him? Go find your man Romeo and have your wicked way with him."

"Um, that's probably like looking up a guy named John Smith back home. I'm guessing there are like a bazillion Francesco Romeos in all of Italy."

"That sounds like a cop-out to me. But if you don't want to have crazy sex with an Italian musketeer, far be it for me to lose sleep over it. I'm just happy to be avoiding my icky date."

"Glad I could be of service."

"Hold on, Allie. I'm gonna put you on speaker for a minute cause I'm Googling this guy. You said he's Francesco Romeo? And he's in Chianti. Where you are?" She was silent for a minute before letting out a loud, low whistle.

"What?" Allie said. She opened up a web browser and typed in Francesco's name. When the page loaded, her eyes widened. "Ho-ly shit." She whistled loudly.

"Right?" her friend said. "I mean, look at that guy. You're not kidding he's hot."

"And that's not even in the musketeer getup."

"And his family owns some huge wine dynasty."

"Wait, he's some rich, famous Italian man?" Allie ran her fingers through her hair. "I'm so out of my league. It's a good thing I bailed before I made a complete fool of myself with him."

"My God, there are a lot of pictures of him with really gorgeous women. Always a different one in every picture. That's a huge red flag, Allie."

Allie let out a growl. "Of course it is," she said. "It figures. Heaven forbid I find a cute, nice, normal guy. Instead I get tangled up with some rich-boy player who has a new hookup every night."

"Yeah. Seriously, while he's drop-dead gorgeous, I'd advise you to turn the other way. You can tell his type. He'll be like all the other guys you've been with: pretty boys with huge egos. Nothing good will come of getting involved with him."

Allie sighed. "I know. It sucks. Maybe I should come

home and go on a date with your blind date. At this rate that's going to be about as good as it gets."

"Trust me, I wouldn't wish him on my worst enemy, let alone my best friend. Now go enjoy your work while you're in Italy. Drink some of that wine you and Lola will be saving from imminent peril, and get that Romeo boy out of your head. Deal?"

Allie nodded. "Deal."

She knew Francesco Romeo would be the absolute worst thing in her life right now, so it was a good thing she wasn't going to have to worry about ever seeing him again.

Chapter Four

FRANCESCO hadn't thought about one niggling little detail when he donned his musketeer outfit: How are you supposed to hide a hard-on when you're wearing tights? It sure made him wonder how male ballet dancers managed that feat, especially when they had their hands all over those hot ballerinas. Because having his own hands on that cute little kitty cat made him rock hard and desperate to find somewhere to hide the undeniable proof of his physiological response until things settled down a bit. Down there.

Seemed like that wasn't going to happen anytime soon, dammit.

"Is that a banana in your man-tights or are you just happy to see me," his eldest brother Alessandro said as he approached him, a glass of wine in his hand. Alessandro had been the sibling who took charge when their beloved father passed away suddenly years ago. The family truly owed it to Sandro for saving the family wine business, which had been run by Romeos for hundreds of years. When their father passed, none of the kids were old enough or at all prepared to run the vast Romeo estate holdings, but Sandro set aside his plans to attend university and not only took over the winery but also served as a surrogate father to his six younger siblings. They all owed him a huge debt of gratitude. Although to be truthful, Sandro could be kind of a bossy asshole about things because of that. And tonight would prove no exception.

"So funny I forgot to laugh," Francesco said, frowning. If anything was going to deplete that erection, it would be his brother giving him a heap of shit.

"Was it the sight of Elettra Giovanetti dressed as a fair maiden that got you all horny?"

Francesco rolled his eyes. "Nothing like an old *nonna* trying to dress like a young princess to buzzkill *that* away." He looked down at his now-diminishing bulge.

"Then come clean, or I'm going to have to tell everyone that you were turned on by wearing women's pantyhose."

Francesco threw him the side-eye.

"Well, if you must know, I met an adorably sexy kitty cat—of the human variety—and let's say we hit it off with a bang. Minus the bang part."

"You work fast, *mio fratello*. You've hardly been at the party for two hours."

"Yes, I've always been far more skilled than you at having my way with women."

"It looks like you didn't quite have your way enough. Otherwise you wouldn't be all alone and 'tenting your tights.'" He made air quotes for emphasis.

"Don't you have some grapes to pick or something?"

"We both know we're not ready to pick yet. But I do hope you have plans in place to deal with those damned birds. Any day now the starlings are going to show up en masse and start feasting on our grapes before we're ready to harvest. Last year, we lost nearly fifty percent of the yield

to those things."

Francesco was more than well aware of that since his brother had been haranguing him nonstop ever since last year's harvest.

"Once our grapes reach fifteen percent sugar, those starlings are going to arrive in droves, and they'll have a three-week head start on when we can pick them—"

"I know, I know. We can't pick until they're at least twenty-one percent sugar. And it's my responsibility to minimize our losses. I get it." Francesco puppeted his words by moving his fingers. "We've been fixing the nets and getting them prepared, but you know netting can only do so much. The barn owl decoys are about to be mounted. We've got the propane-powered cannons serviced and ready to use."

"What about the ground rodents?"

"I've been doing research." Francesco scrubbed his chin with his hand. "Because so far it's a matter of prowling the property and shooing them off, which is obviously not too effective. But with the ground cover we planted, the goal will be to encourage nesting among the vines for carnivorous birds so that they'll be a natural threat to rodents. I'm hoping by next year that will be working well."

"Well, I expect to see some results this year," Sandro said, then pointed at his brother's legs. "Oh, and, what say you put some pants on before you scare your neighbors with that thing."

Francesco snarled his lip. "Thanks, Sandro. I'll be sure to do that," he said as he turned to walk away.

He wandered down terraced steps to the formal Italian garden below and meandered through the maze of low hedges, enjoying the peaceful sounds of the many water fountains in the garden. It gave him time to be alone with his thoughts, which were filled to overflowing with flashbacks of what occurred with that mystery woman, Allie Ledbetter. Damn, that little kitty cat was smoking. He wanted nothing more than to have her lapping at his warm milk. And she seemed to be as into him as he was into her, but then it all came to a screeching halt. He didn't even get her number or any way to get ahold of her. He had no idea where she was from, though he assumed the States, what with the American accent. For all he knew she was leaving Tuscany in the morning. The thought made him sad.

Francesco strolled with his hands behind his back along the harlequin-patterned red-and-white tile path that bisected the garden, admiring the symmetry of the planted beds, the tall cedars on either side of the pathway, and the riotous colors of cultivated flowers. He inhaled the heavy scent of wisteria hanging in the air. A frog sprang in front of his path, and he stopped to stare at the small amphibian. The frog hopped away and Francesco was struck by the impermanence of the thing—much like that ephemeral woman who'd made such a fleeting but resonant impact on him.

He wanted to know who she was. He couldn't simply leave it at that, letting her flee like a scared kitten. But how was he going to find her? Particularly when work demands were about to drag him down like a riptide. Who was he fooling? He wasn't going to have time for women until the grapes were harvested. He might as well put that pussycat right out of his mind for two reasons: first, he'd never find her, and second, his attention was about to shift from sexy felines to pesky birds. Unless he could get that kitty cat to

perform her feline duties and catch thousands of those damned ravenous starlings, it was a moot point anyhow.

Chapter Five

ALLIE always felt as though she looked a bit like a National Park Service ranger in her khaki pants and shirt and the large glove she wore when working with Lola, which made her laugh. Since she'd arrived in Italy, most women she saw were fashionably dressed, not a one in gender-neutral khakis. Rather, they wore style-neutral blacks, grays, and whites. But in her trade, her clothes were for function, not looks. And no doubt her falcon, Lola, was perfectly happy with her lack of fashion savvy as long as she had raw meat treats for her at the ready.

Giovanni had been closely monitoring the Brix, or sugar content, in the grapes to gauge when it would rise to the level at which the birds would start to come in droves before giving Allie the nod to commence with her end of things.

Soon Allie and Lola would be working long days to deter the voracious starlings, which were known to flock in the thousands and could clear a vineyard of its bounty quite rapidly. Today she was going through their daily motions to keep Lola on her toes and had brought her out to the vineyard to practice. Allie removed the bird's hood, and Lola's talons grabbed onto Allie's leather glove. The raptor adjusted her wings as her intelligent brown eyes, reflecting the gold of the sunlight, scanned the horizon and she got her bearings. Soon she flapped her wings, spreading them to their impressive three-foot span, and launched into the air, first circling low over rows of grapes, then lifting upward.

Soon Lola was a tiny dot in the sky, at which point Allie beckoned her back by swinging a lure—a tennis ball with pigeon feathers secured to it attached to a long lead—and calling her with a whistle. With a powerful swoop of her wings, Lola returned to settle on Allie's shoulder, where Allie hand-fed the bird raw quail meat as a reward.

Next Allie prompted the raptor to launch into a series of high-speed dives called "stooping," meant to mimic the capture of winged prey. Allie made sure Lola didn't actually eat any birds she was scaring off; allowing her to eat them in the middle of the workday would take too much time. Hence Allie kept the frozen quail in a pouch around her waist at all times as a reward upon the bird's swift return.

Giovanni pulled up in an *ape*—a three-wheeled commercial vehicle often used on vineyards and farms because it easily negotiated between rows of vines and up steep hills. He got out and stood nearby, watching as Lola performed.

"That's quite an impressive bird," he said, nodding in approval.

"She's pretty amazing. And you're going to be even more impressed with her when you see how much she reduces the starling population."

"I can't wait. In the meantime, are you enjoying yourself here in Chianti?" He placed his hand over his brow to block the sun as he gazed above to watch the falcon advance skyward.

"Of course," she said. "It's beautiful here. And the people are lovely."

"Did you have a good time at the party?"

Allie hoped she wasn't blushing. And hoped too that he didn't see her going at it with that Romeo guy. "It was fantastic."

"I hope you were able to meet some people and weren't too bored."

"In fact, I did chat with one person for a while." She scratched her chin, feigning that she was trying to conjure up his name. "Romeo something or other." *The guy who was about three minutes away from making me come without even touching my nether regions.*

"Ah, you met one of the Romeos? Our mothers are the best of friends."

"I'm trying to remember his first name. Maybe Francesco?" She probably should have been worried about her ability to lie so readily to her boss. It wasn't in her nature.

Giovanni pursed his lips. "Huh. Francesco." He paced back and forth for a minute. "You didn't tell him why you were here, did you?"

She shook her head. "Actually it never even came up in conversation." *We were too busy groping one another to worry about the basics.*

"Excellent," he said. "In case you run into him again while in Tuscany, I'd like for you to refrain from telling him what you're here to do."

She cocked an eyebrow out of curiosity. "Oh?"

He waved his hand. "It's nothing, really. I'm just not sure if he'll appreciate your presence."

She was fairly certain he'd greatly appreciated her

presence, at least until she fled the scene like a spooked racehorse.

"No worries. It'll be our secret. Besides, I'm sure I won't have occasion to see him anymore."

"Perfect." He glanced at his watch and shook his head as if he'd remembered something. "I came out here to see if you'd like to join us at the Calcio this weekend."

"Calcio?"

"It's a crazy sporting event in Florence that originated back in the 1500s as an act of defiance against the Holy Roman Emperor, who had besieged the city. Florentines wanted to show him he hadn't gotten the best of them, that the siege hadn't hurt them, so they decided to showcase this pretty ferocious athletic competition. I mean, why not?"

"Kind of like watching gladiators fight to the death?" She laughed. "Nothing like a good blood sport to get your juices flowing."

"You're not kidding. You've probably heard of *il Palio*, the huge horse race held twice each summer in Siena. Well, this isn't quite on the scale of the Palio, but it involves lots of pomp and circumstance, and they replicate period costumes that would have been worn back in the sixteenth century. It's all about the physical prowess of the men who engage in 'battle.' Though usually stripped down from their costumes—because otherwise, it would be sweltering—they play a pretty aggressive game that's a mixture of soccer, rugby, and wrestling. Maybe a little freestyle boxing too. Add a little cage match for good measure." He stuffed his hands in his pockets. "I think you'll love it."

"So to be clear: I get to go watch hot men wear very little while engaging in sweaty physical activity?" She grinned. "Where can I sign up?"

He laughed. "I thought that would be enticement enough."

"Yeah, well, it sounds like a good way to meet men, so why not?" She shrugged. Not that she was trying to meet men. Especially since she was only a transient resident of Chianti. No sense getting too comfortable with a man she'd never see again.

"You'll certainly get your fill of pageantry and lots and lots of men." He laughed. "I'll be sure to ask my girlfriend if she can introduce you to some of the *calcianti*—the players—preferably before they're bloodied and bruised."

"I'm afraid they might be a bit out of my league," Allie said. "Lest we forget, I'm merely a humble girl who plays with raptors."

"I have a sneaking suspicion you can hold your own. At any rate, we have VIP seats up front. It's a quintessentially Florentine experience—it will truly be like nothing you've witnessed before. By the way, you'll need to dress in bright blue, as we're rooting for the *Azzurro* team."

"My favorite color. In which case I have no reason to miss it." She grinned. "Thanks for including me!"

Chapter Six

THE Calcio Storico Fiorentino falls yearly on the Feast of San Giovanni—otherwise known as Saint John the Baptist—the patron saint of Florence, on the day of the summer solstice. It's a day of huge celebration for Florentines, with parades and parties and of course *the* event of the day, the Calcio.

Naturally once Allie, Giovanni, and his girlfriend entered the city for the celebration, they could see that Florence was a mass of humanity. It was a challenge for Allie to keep up with Giovanni and his girlfriend Letitia as they threaded their way through the crowds, sometimes cutting up through narrow cobbled alleyways to try to circumvent the mobs. It didn't help that she'd never been to this stunning Renaissance city, and all she wanted to do was stare in amazement at the beautiful buildings and architecture. Set against the backdrop of a crisp blue sky punctuated by clouds that looked like fistfuls of cotton balls, they looked spectacular. She could tell she was going to love this town.

A parade of historically costumed participants wended its way through the city en route to Piazza Santa Croce, the site of the final match, which would pit the Bianchi di Santo Spirito against La Santa Croce Azzurri: the white team versus the blue team.

Occasionally as they navigated toward Santa Croce's makeshift field, Allie would stand on her tiptoes to try to view the parade. There were cavalry, crossbowmen, and foot soldiers, displaying an impressive arsenal of medieval-looking weaponry.

The costumes were incredible: women in rich velvet gowns that royalty would have donned five hundred years ago, children in brightly colored pantaloons, and others decorated in their finest riding horses. Cape-adorned men in colorful tights—their heads capped with feathered plumes—banged on drums and played flutes. The colorful marchers cheered and whipped the crowd into a frenzy of excitement.

When they finally arrived at the Piazza Santa Croce, Giovanni ushered the two women toward a fenced-off area reserved for Azzurri supporters and into a sea of azure blue. Besides people dressed in blue from head-to-toe, there were those who'd painted their faces blue as well. Giovanni gave a ticket taker their VIP passes, and they moved toward their seats in the front row.

Allie gazed across the huge piazza, which had been converted into a sandpit, and saw the other half of the spectators all in white. This scene cut quite an imposing line in the sand. The spectacle of color, from parade participants arriving at the field, to fans of both teams, to flag throwers performing on the field before the game, framed by the imposing stark white façade of the Basilica di Santa Croce that loomed over the event like a referee, offered a brilliant jewel box of colors. It was a feast for the eyes.

Giovanni led them into the seats as they shifted and

sucked in their guts and butts while walking past those already seated. Their front-row seats afforded them prime viewing. Evidently it was nice to be the owner of a well-respected Italian vineyard. As they finally sat down, Allie was disappointed that she was seated next to Letitia, who spoke not a word of English. She silently hoped for a game so compelling she wouldn't feel the need to talk to anyone because all around her the conversations and occasional shouts were only in Italian. Several seats to her left were still unoccupied, and perhaps whoever sat next to her on that side might be an English speaker. She could only hope.

The flag throwers were busily doing their flag-tossing thing on the field, and the teams were lining up to enter the field. And Giovanni was quite right—there was nary a shirt among the players—known as calcianti—but damn, they had some good-looking torsos. She didn't speak much Italian, but she knew enough to think they were downright *bellissimo*, although they did look a little bit rough, like one or two might have done a stint in the big house.

Her gaze ventured down from their bare chests and taut abdomens to see them half-costumed in the traditional medieval—or was it Renaissance? Who knew?—pantaloons that she saw on many men in the parade. The Bianchis sported white pantaloons with pomegranate stripes on their thighs, and the Azzuris' bloomers were blue with mulberry stripes.

Fans everywhere were excitedly hurling smoke bombs in the color of their team skyward, and the air was clotted with plumes of blue and white smoke. This game was the final match of a competition that began weeks earlier as a battle between the *quattro quartieri*, the four quarters, which were the historical districts of Florence. But now the teams from Santa Maria Novella and San Giovanni had been eliminated, leaving the remaining two teams in a neighborhood grudge match of sorts, and all of Florence was out in full force to pick a side and celebrate. Allie was so caught up in the excitement around her she failed to notice that someone had arrived to take the seat next to her.

She looked up and instinctively jerked her head away, as if that would keep her from having to acknowledge the man. Because there, before her, stood her musketeer—except this time, he was dressed in a pair of slim-fit jeans that hugged his butt perfectly. She no sooner turned away when she realized that was a completely idiotic move. After all, this man had been fondling her breasts only days earlier, and she'd certainly encouraged that (until she discouraged it). She had to be civil to the guy.

She turned back to him and reached out her hand to shake it as if she was meeting someone for a business luncheon. It figured Francesco leaned over instead and gave her a more intimate two-cheek kiss, the way Italians do when they know one another. And while they didn't exactly know each other, they'd been well on their way, at least in a biblical sense, before she'd regained her senses and put an end to that madness.

"Ciao, Allie," Francesco said. "*Buonna festa di San Giovanni*! And what a beautiful coincidence this is. Here I thought I'd never see you again and it made me so sad, and now we're seatmates together for this amazing Italian spectacle!" He spread his arms out to showcase it.

The idea of the word "mate" being applied to anything to do with her and his royal Romeo hotness sort of made her stomach curl up in knots. Because if she wanted to be real, she had to admit: who wouldn't want to mate with him? He was tall, with broad shoulders, his tight stomach emphasized in his Azzurri T-shirt. And those long, strong legs and that gorgeous ass of his, not to mention his glorious face with that tanned Mediterranean skin tone, those espresso-colored eyes, the sharp lines of his cheekbones, and the sexy scruff on his chin. She had to stop herself from licking her lips. But she so couldn't go there. What happened between them had been an impulsive mistake, and she had to put an end to it pronto.

"Francesco," she said with a curt nod.

"Francesco? That's all I get from you? *Cara*, I thought you would be as happy to see me as I am to see you."

"My name's not Cara. It's Allie."

He gave her a side glance and burst out laughing. "Cara. It means 'dear.' I know your name is Allie. Is there something bothering you?"

It was hard to hear with all the noisemaking going on. Drums banged and someone somewhere blasted one of those obnoxious vuvuzelas, an unfortunate leftover from the soccer World Cup in South Africa, no doubt. Hopefully she could cut Francesco off quickly and get to watching the game, which was about to start.

"Look, Francesco," she said, frowning. "Just so you know, my friend Harper warned me about you."

He squinted his eyes. "Um, your friend Harper? I don't know anyone named Harper. Clearly she doesn't know me. How could she warn you about me?"

"It doesn't matter. Harper doesn't have to know you to know about you."

"What precisely does that mean?"

"You. You're one of those types."

"I can't even begin to understand what type you mean."

"Well, if you don't know what type you are, then I can't help you with that."

"Alrighty, then," he said, squinting his eyes.

"Yep. And just know that I trust Harper."

Right then, a loud cannon went off, announcing the start of the match, which was a perfect opportunity for Allie to switch her focus to the field of play. Although play was perhaps the wrong word. Because lined up facing one another were twenty-seven brutish-looking men per side, their seemingly steroid-enhanced flesh covered in tattoos, their arms puffed out like Popeye after a can of spinach. The men—brutes, really—wasted no time attacking one another and not twenty seconds had passed since the cannon when punches flew, blood spurted, and what looked like chaos unfolded on the field.

Allie looked to one side, which was where Letitia sat, unfortunately—she might have been fine with some hand gestures and maybe some "can you believe this" eye widening, but conversation was not going to happen there. On Letitia's other side, Giovanni, her host, was engrossed in a conversation with the man on his far side, so that was a no-go either.

But she couldn't watch this madness unfolding before her without discussing it with someone! It was as if they were sitting on the sidelines of a war, minus actual weapons. But it seemed certain that within the fifty-minute parameter of this match, surely someone was going to end up dead!

Blue smoke from the ubiquitous flares choked the air and sometimes made it hard to see what exactly was happening on the field. People were screaming for their team, waving blue flags and seemingly ravenous for blood.

Allie was aghast. "This is downright barbaric," she said, breaking her vow of communications chastity with Francesco. "Look at that." She flung her arm toward the field, pointing at a man after he violently attacked another. Some had their opponents pinned in what almost seemed like a homoerotic position: one man flattened to the ground, the other straddling his naked chest. Were it not for the blood gushing from the guy's nose, and the guy on top pressing his hand on the guy's face, one might have thought he had sexual designs on the man beneath him.

"Of course it is. That's what this is all about. Did you not know about this going into it?"

Allie knit her brow. "No, I did not. I was told it was some historic event. I didn't know it was going to be a bloodbath free-for-all."

Nearby on the field of sandy dirt, she saw one man pulling another man's ear as hard as possible, then the other man reach down to bite his bicep. She pointed at it.

"That's not fair!"

"What isn't?"

"Neither of it. You shouldn't be allowed to bite. Or pull on ears."

"Oh, but you can at the Calcio Storico."

"But why?"

Francesco shrugged. "It's the way it's always been done. Pitting man against man. The only rule is you can't kick someone's head. Well, also no double-teaming someone. It's mano a mano, one on one."

"But you can bite and punch and choke and headbutt and elbow each other? And don't they know they'll break their necks headbutting like that?"

"Yeah, in fact in the seventies, one guy bit another one's ear off. The good news is they're also not allowed head-to-head clashes. But I'm afraid violence is part of the game. It's a war game, and it requires violence to win."

"A man's ear got bitten off? What the hell? But why don't they use strategy? Offense and defense. Use guile instead of brawn?"

"They're doing that as well. See, look." Francesco pulled Allie closer to him as he pointed toward a couple of men on the field. "He's trying to open up a hole in his opponent's defense so his teammate can score the goal. If that player tries and misses, then the other team gets a half point."

Just then an Azzurro player threw the ball through the goal and the crowd went wild.

"I think I'm going to cheer for the clock to run fast, so these men don't have to suffer too much."

Francesco laughed. "I am sure they'd appreciate your empathy, but believe it or not, they've trained for this year after year. These men are bloodthirsty."

From where she was sitting Allie could see three players with black eyes already. Another man was bleeding from his ear, and it looked like another one had been racked in his crotch, and he was doubled over in pain.

"They can do that?" she said, pointing at him.

"It's crazy, right? I know I'd not volunteer to submit to such violence. But it's kind of amusing to watch."

"You say amusing. I say horrifying."

"Back when this originated, some five hundred years ago, this was the game of choice for the ruling class. Even popes were said to have played it."

"Well, in that case, if the popes played it, it must be good for you." Allie rolled her eyes.

He held up his hands in surrender. "I'm not defending this necessarily, I'm giving you the background. It's how it's been done. And I think these men fancy themselves modern-day gladiators."

"Well, if it was the sport of the ruling class, I'd say now it's the sport of ex-convicts. I mean look at those guys."

"I'll grant you those men on the field do look pretty rough around the edges."

"Rough around the edges? How about rode hard, put up wet?"

Francesco knit his brow. "I'm not familiar with that term."

She shook her head. "Never mind. At this point, I might be relieved if someone opened a gate to a tunnel behind the doors of the church and let out the lions to finish these fellows off."

Francesco belted out a laugh. "I think a lot of people here would pay good money to witness that."

Allie looked over to see three men being carried off on stretchers. She held up her hand. "Look! People are literally being carried away, and they don't even stop the game. Or the war. Or whatever it is you call this thing."

He shook his head. "Nope. The game lasts fifty minutes, no stoppage for anything."

"What if someone died?"

He laughed. "That seems a bit dramatic. But I don't think they've ever had to consider that."

"You see that one guy? His leg is obviously broken. It's dangling the wrong direction where he's lying on the

stretcher."

Francesco shrugged. "Breaks happen." He grinned at her. "In fact, sometimes all a man needs is a good break."

Chapter Seven

AND man did Francesco need a good break. He wanted so badly to be in Allie's good graces. He couldn't help but be attracted to her. Every time he looked into her golden-hazel eyes, he drowned in them. He kept thinking about the last time he was near that head of blond hair, when his hands were exploring her body while his nose inhaled the intoxicating citrusy scent of her curls. He tried hard not to stare at her breasts, but it was damn near impossible—her blue halter top meant she was without a bra, and those nipples poking at the silky fabric were about killing him.

But he had to play it cool and not let on that he was desperate to get his hands back on her body, *prontissimo*. He hoped the quickest way to achieve that goal was by continuing the conversation with her. The more they talked, the more they shared; the more they shared, the more they could perhaps share in terms of intimacy. At least that was his desperate hope.

"Uh, he's strangling him," Allie said, grabbing Francesco's arm while pointing at a guy who had a serious choke hold on a guy. You couldn't even tell if he was turning blue, what with all the blue smoke filling the air.

"That's okay," Francesco said. "But no sucker-punching. I forgot to mention that earlier."

"Oh, good. As long as it's nothing too violent." She heaved a sigh. "I swear the men being hauled off the field are probably relieved they don't have to be in the death arena any longer."

"Death arena?" He laughed.

"You have to admit this thing brings out the inner troglodyte in these competitors."

"Which is fitting, considering the prize."

"Which is a bath in your opponent's blood?"

"We'll have to suggest that to them for next year," he said with a grin. "The prize is a Chianina cow, one of the oldest cows in existence."

"What the hell are they going to do with that? Eat it alive?"

He laughed again. "Oh it's a symbolic prize—they drag it out for pictures. But after the match they go to the winning neighborhood and ingest massive amounts of bistecca alla fiorentina. So I guess in a way a cow will be eaten tonight, but not the prize cow."

"At least he escapes harm and ritual bloodletting, unlike all of those players."

"They say when Henry the Third of France was staying in Venice, a fight was staged in his honor, and so he concluded the event was 'too small to be a real war and too cruel to be a game.'"

"I'm with Hank. This is a bit morbid for my tastes."

"But all the crazy things that go along with it—those are pretty interesting, no? The costumes, the music, the flags, the parade. I bet you don't get to see things like this back home."

She shook her head. "I can assure you I've never seen anything quite like the spectacle of this event."

He leaned over so Allie could hear him. "To be honest, I'm glad you aren't too into the violence. It would be a little off-putting if you were calling for more blood."

"Glad to be of service."

"Ultimately the biggest prize is bragging rights for an entire year. That's worth its weight in gold with these guys." He pointed to his watch. "The final countdown and the game is done. You can go back home and recover from the trauma of witnessing the violence."

Naturally he wanted nothing more than to bring her back home with him and make her forget all about it.

Suddenly the crowd around them jumped to their feet and roared with anger. Everywhere white confetti started to fall, and even more white smoked filled the air as Bianchi fans tried to storm the field. Players on the field—those who'd survived intact enough to be left standing—were covered in a cement-like muck. Their sweat blended with the dirty sand, and now confetti clung to them. They looked like piñatas that had survived a particularly nasty clubbing.

Francesco could barely see in front of him with all the smoke obscuring his view. Without thinking he reached out and grabbed Allie's hand, pulling her toward the exit.

"Follow me," he said. "I want to make sure you get out of here safely."

Amazingly she didn't tug out of his grip as she followed him out, bumping into people and stepping on a few feet amidst the mayhem. At last they were on the street.

"My God, that was terrifying," she said. The hand he held was shaking. She turned to look behind her then froze. "Giovanni? Giovanni!" A look of worry spread across her face and she scoured the crowd. "I have no idea where my friend is. He's my ride back."

"No worries, I'll make sure you get back safely."

"But I came with him and his girlfriend. That would be rude. They'll worry about me."

"Text him and let him know. In this crowd you'd be hard-pressed to find him. It's a crazy scene here. And you can see *i Bianchi* are starting to get whipped into a frenzy. You don't want to go back toward that at this point."

She pursed her lips. They were walking into a thick crowd of Bianchi fans, all dressed in white. Some were jeering at her. Francesco pulled her off to the side.

"Here," he said, letting go of her hand for a minute to pull his shirt over his head. Beneath his blue shirt was a white one, which he also pulled off. "Take this." He pulled it over her head and helped her slip her arms into the sleeves.

"You wore two shirts today?"

He grinned. "I figured I'd hedge my bets. That way I could have fun celebrating either team's victory since I've got friends on both sides."

Her eyes grew wide. "I have to admit, that's rather brilliant."

He shrugged. "I'll take a compliment from you any way I can get it."

"But now what are you going to do?"

He folded his blue shirt up and set it atop a nearby trash receptacle. "I'll go shirtless. Maybe they'll mistake me for a calciante and treat me like a hometown hero."

She shook her head. "Are you kidding? You're far too good-looking to be mistaken for one of those rough-and-tumble players." She blushed and frowned. "By that I mean you aren't bruised and bloodied like they are."

"At any rate, I'm good to go shirtless today. Enough men are doing that, so I'll hardly be noticed. And if I find a place to pick up a white Bianchi team shirt, I'll grab one." He pointed at her. "But you might want to consider removing that halter top beneath because the blue is showing through."

"Really? You think that will matter, like I'll be run out of town?"

"Well, we're going into the heart of Bianchi territory, to the Piazza Santo Spirito, where things will be crazy wild. Maybe you shouldn't take a chance."

Of course Francesco had an ulterior motive—if the blue showed through, which it did slightly, then without that shirt, he might get an even better show.

"Okay. If you think so," she said, as she unhooked the fastener at her neck and deftly squirmed the top off while still wearing the white shirt. "You sure this isn't too see-through?"

He shook his head, suppressing a wolfish grin. "Not at all. It looks great. And an impressive thing, taking off that top without exposing any body parts." Although he'd have loved to see those parts exposed.

He couldn't believe this stroke of good fortune: not only did Allie Ledbetter practically fall from the blue into his lap, but now she also willingly went braless at his behest. Things were finally looking up.

Chapter Eight

MAYBE Harper wasn't altogether right in her assessment. After all, Francesco seemed to be quite the chivalrous gentleman. Here he quite literally gave her the shirt off his back to keep people from jeering at her. How sweet was that? And then even urged her to remove her blue halter top from beneath, since the blue was still obvious through the white of the shirt covering it. He didn't have to do that. He was protecting her. It seemed like an awfully kind gesture.

And the upside to this shirt switcheroo was that she could steal glances at Francesco's gorgeous golden pecs, which were covered with the right amount of dark hair that trickled down to his tight abs. She was drawn to that location like iron filings to a magnet. Because below the edge of his waistband, that taunting little happy trail led to what she already knew—by the mere feel of it the other night—was a very special treat.

Good Lord. How was she going to keep her hands to herself?

Once again Francesco reached for her hand and gave it a tug, encouraging her to join him. They followed a massive processional of Bianchi players and fans toward their destination across the Arno River in the area known as the

Oltrarno, to the Piazza Santo Spirito, the home turf for the team.

"Have you ever been to *Firenze* before?"

Allie shook her head.

"Well, then we're going to divert by way of the Duomo because you must get a glimpse of that up close and personal." He turned right as the parade of people streamed toward the river, and they walked another five minutes until the imposing cathedral towered in front of them.

Allie's eyes were wide. "That is the most spectacular building I think I've ever seen," she said as she beheld the red, green, and white marble edifice topped by the famous dome designed by Filippo Brunelleschi in the fifteenth century.

"It's a masterpiece of beauty and engineering. And as massive as it is, it blends in well with the architecture of the city," he said. "I'd love to take you inside, but today is not the day to tour the Duomo with the throngs of tourists here. Earlier today, during the Duomo's parade, the priests carried church relics from the cathedral to the Baptistery across the piazza." He pointed to the octagonal building nearby.

"Relics?"

"Oh, Italian churches love to keep supposed bits of body parts of saints and such. Fingers, toes, hair clippings. I guess it's a religious fetish."

Allie scrunched her nose. "That sounds almost as disgusting as that bizarre man-battle we witnessed back there."

"Except with the church, it's much more civil. They usually keep them in intricate silver urns and such."

"Oh, in that case." She giggled.

"Perhaps we can come back another day and climb to the top and wait till the church bells chime, something I love to do."

"I'd enjoy that," Allie said, surprising even herself with that reply.

"In the meantime let's get to the festivities." They walked along the busy Via dei Calzaiuoli, admiring fashions in store windows and various food and pastries on display in others, then cut back toward the river, crossing the Ponte Santa Trinita.

"I wanted to take you across this bridge because that way you get a much better view of the famed Ponte Vecchio, the bridge with the secret passageway above it that allowed the Medici noblemen to cross the river Arno without ever having contact with common people." He pointed to the bridge, which glowed with the golden warmth of the early evening sunlight.

They stopped midway across the bridge and sat on the stone railing, admiring the view of Florence and the river that their vantage point afforded them.

"I can't believe how breathtaking this place is," she said. "So much history and beauty."

"And there's more to see." Francesco held up his finger. He took her hand and they stood to leave. "But first an important stop."

At the far end of the bridge, he led her into a gelateria. "We are officially in the Oltrarno, the far side of the River Arno. And this, in my humble opinion," he said, pointing to a storefront they were approaching, "has hands down the best gelato in town."

Allie looked at the sign, which read Gelateria Santa

Trinita. "Finally! This is my first gelato since I got to Italy. My friend Harper—"

Francesco interrupted. "You mean Harper who doesn't like me yet doesn't even know me?"

Allie winced. "One and the same. Harper told me I had to go to a real gelateria, not one of those tourist traps that have neon-colored gelato piled high in the refrigerator case."

"Your friend is wise about some things, at least," he said. "Behold." He extended his arm out to showcase the gelato options as they entered the shop. "I would highly recommend the *sesamo nero*, which sounds weird—black sesame—but it tastes divine. And for your second scoop, I'd go for the aptly named Santa Trinita. Trust me, you'll thank me."

"When in Rome, I guess," Allie said as she placed her order. "Make that when in Florence."

They walked as they ate their gelato, going past antique stores and art galleries. White sheets and large Bianchi flags were draped everywhere from the windows above; they waved in the gentle evening breeze.

"Damn, they really do get into this, don't they?"

Francesco laughed. "I'd say that's an understatement. But that reminds me—I should probably pick up a white shirt once we get over to the piazza. I'm sure there will be vendors selling them."

The last thing Allie wanted was for that beautiful torso to be covered with a shirt. She was enjoying taking in that sight as much as the architectural ones. In fact, one look at him in the air-conditioned gelateria and she shivered, noticing his nipples had hardened from the chill. It made her want to drag her tongue along them and maybe keep moving farther down his chest.

"I think you shouldn't even bother," she said. "Think of all the women you'll attract this way." She winked at him. Granted using this ploy was a gamble; she sure as hell didn't want to compete for his attention with the many beautiful Italian women nearby.

He cocked his eyebrow. "You make a good point."

"Absolutely," she said, playing along as she took a swipe of her gelato with her tongue. "I've seen women giving you the once-over as we've been walking."

Francesco stopped and pointed at his chest. "You're serious? You think women are ogling me?"

"Well, they might find you more appealing with, say, thigh-high leather boots and tights. Maybe that feather in your cap, but barring that, I'd say skins versus shirts win every time."

"You liked my thigh-high boots, did you?"

She laughed. "I told Harper I had serious boot envy."

"There you go invoking the all-knowing Harper again. What is her deal? Why doesn't she like me—even though she doesn't know me?"

Allie scrunched her nose. "I don't know." She was way too embarrassed to get into this. It would suggest she had investigated him after she fled the party, and that admission would be mortifying.

"What do you mean you don't know? You must know something."

Allie held up her hands in surrender. "Okay, fine. If you insist." She heaved a sigh, thrusting out her lower lip in a pout. She so didn't want to go there. "After the party, I went back to where I'm staying, and oh, I don't know, I was feeling conflicted."

"Conflicted?" He lifted his brow.

"Are you going to make me confess all of my sins?"

"There is a church nearby if that helps." He pointed toward the Basilica di Santo Spirito.

"Ha ha. Very funny." She threw him a side glance. "I wasn't sure what was the right thing for me to do."

"About?"

She rolled her eyes. "Must I spell it out? About us. Or it. Or what happened. However you want to say it."

He grinned and she hated that he did because he had this dimple on his right cheek that made her want to drag her tongue along that too, dammit.

"I ended up calling Harper, who is my best friend, because she has good radar."

"Radar?"

Allie shook her head. "Just about every time I've ever dated a guy, she's warned me that he's was bad news." She paused and caught herself and pointed first at him, then at herself. "Oh, God. Not that you and I were dating. Obviously not. I didn't mean dating per se. What I meant is, like, we had some sort of something. Ugh, that doesn't sound right, does it? You know what I'm saying. But anyhow, she would always warn me about a guy I was attracted to, and she was always right. But I never listened to her."

Francesco was laughing. "I'm rather enjoying this."

He took a bite of his cone, and she saw his tongue reaching to catch a piece of cone as it crumbled, and her heartbeat sped up. That tongue. In her mind, she replayed the moment their tongues touched at the costume party. She noticed a piece of cone fell into the hair on his chest and she froze, staring at it. And then she did exactly the thing she knew she shouldn't do: she reached over and pulled the bit of sticky gelato-drippy cone from his chest and popped it into her mouth.

Francesco's eyes grew wide. And her face turned hot. *Jesus. What the hell did I do that for?*

She tried to mentally placate herself that at least she didn't clean it off his chest with her mouth. But that was slight consolation. She literally ate a sticky piece of a cone from his heart-stoppingly sexy chest. That was no way to avoid further sexually charged encounters with a man she'd love to have another sexually charged encounter with. Crap.

Chapter Nine

FRANCESCO felt as if his life's work was done now that he had Allie Ledbetter practically eating off of his chest. Only thing better would have been if she had eaten it off an even more willing body part. But maybe they could work on that. Nevertheless, the mere thought of what she did meant she was interested, which was good. When she'd left so abruptly from the party, it was impossible to read her and figure out what the hell was going through her mind. Maybe she was conflicted. Something to do with past lovers or lack of trust. With these few little bread crumbs to follow, he now had hope that he could crack this code.

But first he had to help her not feel uncomfortable about what she'd done. The pink that tinged her cheeks told him she was embarrassed. He figured the best way to deflect it was with a little humor.

What he honestly wanted to do was break off a piece of the cone and let it drop onto her breasts, which he could make out fairly well through his thin, white shirt. He would happily eat every last crumb from there. For that matter, he'd gladly put the crumbs directly on her breasts and cut to the chase, licking and sucking all of it off of her. But that would need to wait. Instead, he offered up his cone.

"Still hungry?" he said with a grin, tipping his cone

toward Allie.

She rolled her eyes for what seemed the tenth time today. "Sorry. That was weird of me. I don't know what I was thinking."

He held up his hands. "No worries. I'm happy I could have been of assistance. But you better save some room because you'll be feasting at this celebration."

"Seriously? I thought we were just wandering around. I didn't know we were going to the dinner. How did you get an invite?"

"I have friends in high places."

The crowd was getting thick as they approached the Piazza Santo Spirito, which was awash in a sea of white-garbed humans. The sound of the talking and cheering and shouting was as loud as a busy nightclub, yet here it was in the open air. On either side of the piazza, there were two buffet tables and long lines of people stood behind them. Down the center was another buffet line reserved for the calcianti, who were enjoying the spoils of victory: all the bistecca alla fiorentina—a grilled steak dish famous in Florence—they could eat. The Bianchi were seated at two long tables, their meal continually disrupted by well-wishers congratulating them.

"I'd like you to meet someone," Francesco said as he led Allie toward the players.

"Oh, no. Let's not interrupt them. They're having a good time. Plus they're so dirty and sweaty, and, well, bloody."

It was true. The men basked in their glory covered in the evidence of their hard-fought victory: dried blood, sweat-caked sand and dirt, cuts, bruises, black eyes, slings. It was as if they had come home from war.

"Not to worry," he said. "It's worth getting a little dirty for. After all, how often will you be able to say you celebrated with the winners of the Calcio?"

As they walked toward the players, one man looked at them and stood, arms extended. "Francesco Romeo! *Ciao amico mio.*" He enveloped Francesco in a bear hug.

"*Congratulazioni*, Fabrizio," Francesco said, extending his arm toward Allie. "I'd like you to meet my friend Allie Ledbetter. Allie, this is Fabrizio Trapunto, proprietor of one of my favorite restaurants in Firenze, Trattoria di Santo Spirito. Oh and survivor and victor of the Calcio."

Fabrizio opened his arms wide and reached out for Allie, lacing his arms around her tightly and lifting her off the ground with his zeal. He placed her earthward and gave her a strong once-over, first whistling.

"*Bellissima*," he said, drawing out the word for emphasis, then nodding with approval. "You are most beautiful." He kept nodding and leaned toward Francesco. "*Parla Italiano?*"

He wanted to know if she spoke Italian.

Francesco shook his head.

"Va bene." All right. "Ha una splendida serie di tette."

Francesco suppressed a laugh since Fabrizio just said she had a gorgeous set of tits. Thank God Allie didn't speak Italian because she'd probably have slapped him. He could only imagine the brawl that would ensue afterward. Not only that, but she'd realize how spectacular her tits looked in that skimpy white T-shirt she was wearing. He wanted to continue to savor stealing peeks at those things without her being the wiser. Plus she'd be ticked at him if she knew how freaking amazing they looked, with her hard nipples pressing against the thin fabric, since he'd talked her out of her halter top, quite literally.

"*Sono spettacolari, vero?*" Francesco said to him. They're quite spectacular, aren't they?

"*Mi piacerebbe succhiarli.*" He winked at Francesco and slapped him on the back, laughing, as he told him in Italian that he'd love to suck on them.

"*Mi dispiace, ma sono miei,*" Francesco said. Sorry, but they're mine. He sure as hell hoped they would be. Which meant he'd better get Allie away from his friend before she got wind of their conversation.

"Enjoy your celebration, my friend," Francesco said as he slapped him on the back and they said goodbye.

"What was he saying to you back there?" Allie asked as they waited in line for food.

"Oh, nothing," Francesco said. "Well he said you were beautiful, and we talked about the match for a second."

"You sure that's it?" she said. "Because he had this lecherous look in his eyes."

He shrugged. "Put a man in a death match for fifty minutes and see if you won't notice all sorts of inappropriate emotions painted on his face. It does things to a man."

She shook her head. "I guess. But ugh, hugging him was a little much." She looked down at her shirt that had picked up streaks of blood and dirt from his bare chest. "Hope you didn't want to keep this shirt."

"Sorry about that. I'd rub it off on my chest, but that might be weird to do in public here. Though it would feel incredible." He cocked his eyebrow at her.

"Just because something feels good doesn't mean you should follow through on your urges to do it."

Francesco tapped her nose with the tip of his finger.

"Sometimes you never know until you try." He handed her a plate, and they took servings of lasagna al forno and several side dishes. He led her to a nearby fountain where she sat on the edge while he went to a nearby bar to buy some wine.

When he returned, he handed her a glass of wine and tipped his glass to it. "*Salute*," he said. "You know I still don't even know what you're doing here in Italy, where you're staying, any of that."

"Oh, I'm simply enjoying the Tuscan countryside," she said. "Staying with some friends of friends. I was looking to get away for a little bit and someone suggested this."

He nodded. "That's a nice friend to hook you up like that."

Although he hoped she wasn't hooking up with whomever she was staying with.

"Yeah, it seems to be working out," she said. She looked around the piazza with all the people partying and laughing and eating and drinking. "All of this, so a bunch of men can go behave like primitive animals for fifty minutes?"

"It's much more than that. First off, the Calcio is the precursor to the game of football—what you Americans call soccer—and what we call the 'beautiful game.' Everybody loves soccer, and the Calcio takes on this local lore as being the grandfather of our national pastime. But in addition to that, these groups do much to build community. They organize events for charity, hold big blood drives, visit sick children in the hospital. All sorts of things to shore up local support. This *campanilismo*—the sense of loyalty to their local church tower, or *campanile*, referring to their neighborhood, is emblematic of how important it is to the players to keep their tight-knit communities bonded."

"Okay, that's encouraging. At least it's not all about blood sacrifice."

"The calcienti are local heroes to many, and it's often a tradition passed down from father to son. My friend Flavio Selvaggio is with Azzurro. I know that he and his team, which is comprised of far more players than will be on the pitch during the match—maybe close to sixty total— practice hours at a time, three times a week for three months leading up to the quarterfinals and finals. All this to play at best two games."

"My bet is their bodies couldn't take more than two games the way they go at it."

He nodded. "There's a reason that it didn't rise to the level of popularity that football has. Plenty enough injuries in that sport as it is. Sure, to the outsider, it seems a bit brutish, but I guess I'd say it's complicated."

"I suppose that's not the only complicated thing in the world."

He tipped his head and looked at her. "Though sometimes, perhaps we complicate things more than we need to."

And with a little luck, maybe he could simplify whatever it was between them that had gotten stuck, and they could pick up where they last left off.

Chapter Ten

ALLIE was relieved to have changed the conversation so that she didn't have to outright lie to Francesco. It was awkward enough not to own up to her real reason for being in Tuscany, but she felt as if she had to honor her host's request. This act of omission became particularly uncomfortable because she was enjoying herself with Francesco. He was funny and handsome and kind and generous. After all, he'd dropped everything to spend the evening with a complete stranger today. Well, not exactly a complete stranger. He was, after all, relatively familiar with parts of her body. Which made her insides sizzle at the mere memory of his hands on her breasts. God, so close yet so far—albeit all of her own wimpy doing.

A band was playing music on another end of the piazza, and once they finished eating, Francesco stood up, dusted his palms off on his jeans, and extended his hand to help Allie stand.

"Would you care to dance?" he asked.

"I'd like nothing more." Her own words surprised her.

They walked hand in hand toward the music. Once they reached the edge of the crowd of people dancing, Francesco pulled her tightly into his embrace as they swayed to the music. Allie caught her breath; being this close to his warm flesh made her heart race. How could it be that days ago she fled the embrace of this man and right now, she'd probably have a hard time saying no if he stripped her naked and had his way with her right here, in front of all these people. Had she lost her mind?

No. Her mind was perfectly sound and she was happy exactly where she was, with Francesco's strong, shirtless chest pressed up against her braless breasts. It was about as close as they were going to get in a public piazza, and it would have to do. Francesco's hands rested low on her hips and gently guided her pelvis toward the unmistakable hard-on she was pressed up against. She let herself sink into the warmth of his solid body against hers. Soon he was whispering sweet nothings in Italian into her ear. She had no idea what any of the words meant, but she knew how it felt—erotic and sensual.

"*Cara mia*," he murmured. "*Sei così bellissima.*" My dear. You are so beautiful. He was practically purring at her now and man, did she wish she spoke fluent Italian because whatever he was saying, it sounded amazing.

His lips nuzzled the edge of her ear as he continued to whisper coaxing words. "*Mi fai eccitare. Voglio fare l'amore con te.*" You turn me on. I want to make love to you.

Who knew all it took were a bunch of meaningless words to get her hot and bothered? And by bothered, she could feel her panties dampening with each utterance from his mouth.

"*Voglio sentirti sulla mia pelle.*" I want to feel you on my skin. "*Voglio farti gemere di piacere.*" I want to make you moan with pleasure. Francesco traced his tongue along Allie's ear, alternating kisses with gentle strokes of his tongue, all the while talking dirty to her in Italian. "*Voglio essere sepolto*

profondamente dentro di te." I want to be buried deep inside of you.

It was all gibberish to Allie, but it was the sexiest gibberish she had ever encountered. Maybe it was his hard length pressed against that perfect juncture, or maybe it was his hands, which took possession of her body as if it was his birthright. Who knew? But it was working. Allie relaxed into him, burying her nose in his neck, inhaling the tantalizing scent of his own sweat combined with some sort of woodsy aftershave, hinting at cedar and citrus. It was a good thing she was in the middle of a public venue or she'd no doubt have allowed him to urge her up against a wall with her legs around his waist and his cock pressed deep inside her wet warmth.

But then she remembered Harper and those photographs of Francesco with his many women *du jour*, and all those idiot men she was happy to sleep with once upon a time, only to realize they were self-absorbed duds uninterested in anything more than a quickie or two. And so when the song ended, she separated from Francesco, all those sexy Italian words be damned.

"I think I need to find the ladies' room," she said, averting his gaze.

Francesco knit his brows but took a step back, taking a deep breath. "Yeah. The toilet. Um, can you give me a second and I'll take you there?"

Well, if that wasn't awkward. Nothing like standing in a piazza packed to overflowing with people while basically grinding into the woman you want but evidently can't have, only to get the kiss-off and be left standing with a serious hard-on that tested the limits of the stitch strength on your jeans. But there you have it. He couldn't figure out what was up but she had this mental cock-block thing going, and he had no idea how to cock-block her cock-block, which was making him nuts.

He ushered her away from the piazza, avoiding the crowd, and at last found a restaurant owned by some friends, who kindly let her use their bathroom.

Like any good general in charge of a delicate military operation, Francesco knew that if one strategy failed, he merely needed to reconnoiter. After all, he'd practically had her eating out of the palm of his hand until something stirred regret or warning in her head. He would have to get into her head enough to circumvent whatever that was. No problem.

They retraced their path to the river, crossing over the same bridge. Clouds of saffron-tinged meringue painted the sky with a uniquely Florentine color that hinted at sunset—the kind that stole your breath away.

"I wanted to cross this way again because you get a lovely perspective of the repeating bridges along the Arno. Plus the deeper the melon color of the evening sky, the more beautiful the Ponte Vecchio looks illuminated with the natural colors from the light."

He hitched himself over the edge of the railing onto a ledge that jutted out from the bridge and helped Allie scoot over the railing as well. One woman sat against the bridge, engrossed in a book. Another couple enjoyed a bottle of wine. They sat there, legs dangling over the edge, admiring the view in silence for a while.

"This is the oldest elliptic arch bridge in the world. It was first built in the sixteenth century. Sadly the retreating German army destroyed it during World War II. But the bridge was eventually rebuilt with original stones raised from the Arno, and the statues depicting the Four Seasons were returned to their corners. Eventually the missing head of the Primavera statue was recovered from the riverbed and returned to her rightful place as well."

"You know so much about this city."

"I consider myself a Florentine at heart," he said. "My family has our vineyard in Chianti, but we have straddled both places: the Cantine dei Marchesi Romeo and Palazzo Romeo here in Firenze."

Her eyes grew wide. "You have a palace in this city? Must be worth a fortune."

He laughed. "No doubt, but we're not selling it anytime soon and haven't concerned ourselves with its value."

"Do you stay there when you're in the city?"

"At times. But I keep a private apartment here as well. It depends on whether I want to embroil my family in my comings and goings." He smiled. He most definitely wouldn't dare complicate the tenuous state of whatever this burgeoning relationship with Allie Ledbetter was by daring to subject her to the intrusiveness of his family. His sister alone would have a field day and never let him live it down. Time to change the subject.

"What do you think of this beautiful city so far?"

"It's like nothing I've ever seen," she said. "Not that I've seen much. I mean I've seen plenty in the States, what with—"

She pursed her lip.

"What with what?"

She shook her head. "Oh, nothing. I don't know what I was saying."

"About your travels back home?"

"Yeah, I've road-tripped quite a bit back home. But it's nothing like this. Italy is so steeped in history and tradition. It's truly remarkable."

"Well, I'm spoiled, but I do agree with you. We have an enviable culture that dates back many centuries. My family alone has been making wine for over six hundred years. Our roots reach back to the days of Italian nobility and the famed house of Savoy. In fact we have immediate ties to the royals of neighboring Monaforte as well, as my uncle Enrico, Duke of Santo Miele, is married to that country's Queen Ariana."

"Wow, you're royalty?" she shook her hand, teasing him as if he was too hot to touch.

"Ish. My eldest brother, Alessandro, carries the title Marchese Alessandro Romeo, but honestly, we all tend to downplay that archaic terminology except when necessary at official events where the cachet of the royal title helps with the family business. Or in the case of Sandro, when it used to help him pick up beautiful women. That was before he settled down with Taylor McFarland."

"Wait a minute. Your brother is with the famous American model Taylor McFarland?"

He shrugged. "In a family as large as mine, beautiful women tend to come and go with regularity, so I never get into the habit of seeing them as anything more than the people they are. Taylor happened to stick around. Don't get

me wrong—I love Taylor a great deal. I don't view her as someone famous but rather view her as part of the family."

"You are quite the international man of mystery, I will say." Allie shook her head and looked at him with a hint of confusion in her eyes.

"Pot meet kettle, cara," he said. Because he'd never met a more intriguing and reticent woman. And damned if that didn't make him want to delve more, despite how vexing he found her at times.

Chapter Eleven

IF anything could further cement in Allie's mind that she was far, far removed from the world of Francesco Romeo, it was that his family was royalty. And his brother was with Taylor McFreakingFarland.

She tried for a minute to mentally put herself on the same pedestal as the famous supermodel, but it only made her cringe to fathom it. With her generous curves and relatively diminutive five-feet-six-inch height, she certainly was not ever going to be the statuesque beauty that Taylor was. Nor would she be famous. Nor would she be sought for her pulchritude. Nor would she be as rich. Or even remotely financially comfortable. She was seriously out of her league.

But in some ways that was good to know. Because now she could step back and be friendly with Francesco without entertaining the notion that the two of them could somehow be an item. Francesco was going to end up with one of those many women who decorated his arm in the tabloids Harper unearthed. Allie felt foolish imagining she ever had a chance in the rarified world that the Romeos occupied.

"Are you ready to continue on your private tour of Florence?"

Allie nodded. "There's more? I really should start thinking of getting back."

"Are you kidding me? We're only getting started."

Allie squinted at him, suspicious. Did he have something nefarious up his sleeve? Granted she'd practically dry-humped the man on the dance floor. And sure, he masterfully fondled her breasts at her shameless behest. But she didn't exactly know him. And here she was gallivanting around the city with him. Then again, didn't he mention that his mother was best friends with Giovanni's mother? In which case, there's no way he could be a serial killer. Besides, with that chest? She closed her eyes against the thoughts of how right it felt to have her breasts pressed against that beautiful chest of his, the soft scratch of his chest hair against her skin. And how much she'd love to have no layer of fabric—thin as it was—between the two of them. The idea of that almost took her breath away.

Yet the truth was, if anything, he was a serial womanizer. And she'd already solved that problem: she was simply going to employ willpower to steer clear of whatever attempts he might make to woo her yet again. She was wise to the prize and had to remind herself that she was never going to be the likes of Taylor McFarland. Best to put that notion to rest right now.

Francesco helped her off the ledge and over the side of the bridge, onto the sidewalk. They crossed the bridge back into Florence proper, then walked along the river, turning left at the Ponte Vecchio. There they could see the throngs of tourists on the famous bridge, many looking to purchase the gold jewelry it was famous for while others were there only for the experience.

"We can go on there later when it's less crowded,"

Francesco said. "I've got something much more pleasant in mind."

They walked for several more minutes until they reached the wide-open Piazza della Signoria filled with beautiful sculptures and plenty of tourists.

Francesco led the way, steering through crowds of sightseers, past cafes where people sat enjoying cocktails or meals.

"Welcome to one of my favorite piazzas, the Piazza della Signoria." He spread his arms wide to showcase it, then pointed at a large fountain. "Some high points of the piazza include the Fontana del Nettuno," he said. "The Fountain of Neptune. It was a vanity project of Cosimo I de'Medici. He held a contest to design a fountain at the same time a new aqueduct was being built, which marked the first time the city would have running water. The statue features Neptune in a chariot drawn by seahorses. It's probably no coincidence that the face of Neptune greatly resembled that of Cosimo. To spruce it up a bit, the sculptor threw in reclining bronze river gods and laughing satyrs. Then for good measure, statues of Scylla and Charybdis."

"This Cosimo guy sounds ambitious. I like his fountain, though!"

"Ahh, Cosimo. Yes, he was quite. Became the first Grand Duke of Tuscany. He proudly ushered in the new golden age for Florence. He was a huge patron of the arts and brought us the glorious Uffizi Gallery." He pointed in front of them. "He restored the Medici family back to power and finished the sprawling Pitti Palace and the sumptuous Boboli Gardens in the Oltrarno."

He indicated a statue right before them. "And here you

have the fake David, in front of the building we are going to enter. The fake David is a replica of Michelangelo's *David*, which used to stand here but now is actually in the Galleria dell'Accademia, about ten minutes from here." He pointed to the building in front of them; it looked like a castle with its imposing crenellated walls. "The Palazzo Vecchio is Florence's town hall, built during the medieval era and still used as such. I'm partial to the statues right across from here." He pointed toward a building adjoining the Uffizi Gallery, beneath a series of wide arches open to the piazza.

Allie turned to see where he was motioning. There were so many works of art to take in, and this was only out in the piazza. She couldn't imagine what works were held behind the walls of the famous gallery.

"This is my favorite statue," Francesco said. "Perseus holding up Medusa's severed head in his hand. It's pretty impressive, this bronze with blood appearing to gush from the head and neck of the dead Medusa. Also here is the famous *Rape of the Sabine Women*—made from one imperfect block of white marble—the largest ever transported to Florence. The figures in the statue form a spiral movement you can see from all sides. But enough of discussing artwork. We're here for the view." He pointed to the top of the building. "You see there, Arnolfo's Tower? At three hundred some feet, it's the highest point in the city other than the Duomo. That, cara, is our destination."

She arched her brow in a "you've got to be kidding me" look. Nevertheless, he directed her to the building, escorting her past the fake David and into an interior courtyard of marble and Corinthian columns and arches with yet another impressive fountain. He then hastened her to the stairs, past the fresco-filled massive Salone dei Cinquecento, the Hall of Five Hundred, where they began their ascent, scaling the narrow steps higher and higher.

"I would definitely have worn my tennis shoes if I knew I was going to be climbing a mountain today," Allie said.

"It'll be worth your efforts. Trust me."

They reached the battlement patrol path, where they could look past the crenellations to see a breathtaking view of the city as the sun was quickly descending.

"Ah, but we have a little farther to climb," he said, steering Allie toward the tower. They continued to mount the stairs, finally wending around a spiral staircase, to behold the setting titian Tuscan sun, ablaze with brilliance, casting its tangerine glow over the city, and highlighting the burnished clay tile rooftops. Cotton candy-pink clouds billowed in the sky as the sun cast its long shadows across the city.

"Well?" Francesco said, his eyes wide with anticipation.

Allie shook her head. "Francesco Romeo, you have truly outdone yourself. This is beyond breathtaking. It's truly magical. I can't believe I'm standing here, on top of the world, overlooking the most beautiful and romantic city on the planet."

He grinned. "Paris might challenge you on that assignation."

"Well, Paris can argue all they want. But this"—she spread her arms in amazement—"this is like nothing I've ever seen."

"The good news is I have one more trick up my sleeve for you tonight."

"Before I turn into a pumpkin at midnight?"

"We'll try to avoid letting your footmen turn into mice."

"I wish I could stay up here all night."

"At least we're not yet done—like I said, I've got one more surprise in store. I think you'll like that as well."

Allie couldn't imagine what else he had planned, but damn, she was finding it harder by the minute not to succumb to the man's immense charms.

Chapter Twelve

THE two walked a few blocks to the Cantinetta dei Romeo.

"Uh, I'm guessing by the name Cantinetta dei Romeo this is owned by your family?" Allie said, standing back to take in the café.

"Just a little place to showcase our wines in the city. A fun project we took on a few years ago. We included a bakery and we offer an *aperitivo* menu, nothing too fancy. Now, for our purposes, we're going to get a few items for our next destination."

Allie was terribly curious about what he had in store for her. She watched as Francesco spoke in rapid Italian. Oh, that language—it practically made her panties wet just hearing it. To think he wasn't even whispering things into her ear and it still had that effect on her.

The woman behind the counter loaded up a bag with several items and with a few ciaos and *a presto*s to say farewell, they left the little Romeo wine showcase and worked their way back in the direction of the river.

When they arrived at the river, they came to a tall, honey-gold six-story building close to the Ponte Vecchio. A doorman greeted Francesco by name, which interesting. Was this some hotel of sorts where he brought all of his women? Well, Allie certainly wasn't going to be one of *them.*

They strolled through the contemporary marble-filled lobby decorated in subtle monochromatic whites and grays, past a terrace that overlooked the water, where people gathered over cocktails. Francesco steered Allie to an exit sign, which led to a staircase going down. They took the steps two by two until they reached the bottom level, where he opened a door onto a grassy lawn right on the banks of the river. Allie glanced around and here and there were a handful of couples, all seemingly lost in their respective conversations. No one even turned to look at them.

"Wow," she said. "Your own private beach?"

He grinned. "Sort of." He opened the bag and pulled out what looked to be a tablecloth, and he spread it out across the grass. "I thought this would be a nice place to have a late-evening picnic."

Allie couldn't believe it. He'd sneakily picked up supplies for their private picnic and brought her to this exclusive site. So it wasn't a ploy to bed her like all of those women he was in the pictures with after all. What a relief.

"Francesco," she said, shaking her head in disbelief. "You don't cease to amaze me with your fantastic plans. We've done more in one evening in Florence than most people do in a year!"

"I aim to please, signora," he said, offering for her to sit on their makeshift blanket. "Maria gave me another tablecloth to use as a blanket in case we get cold. Let's sit on this, and we can spread out the picnic next to us with the other one."

Lights had come on in the city and on the storied bridge nearby; the Ponte Vecchio was reflected in the still waters of the river, and it felt downright magical.

He pulled out two champagne flutes and popped the cork on a bottle of sparkling *rosato* from Romeo estates. Then he pulled out some Tuscan bread, a small bottle of olive oil, some pecorino and *parmiggiano* cheese, and slices of prosciutto.

"I apologize we don't have chairs, but I figured we could make do, considering the impulsive nature of this picnic," he said, smiling.

"Don't be silly. This is truly perfect. I can't believe what a wonderful day it's been. And all because I lost my host."

"His loss, my gain."

They sat, eating and chatting and then Allie was startled by a loud sound. A brilliant pink light overtook the sky.

"Oh, my God. You're kidding me. Fireworks?"

"Made to order, cara," Francesco said.

"You knew all along we were going to see fireworks and you didn't let on?" She playfully hit him on the arm.

"Of course. *Come si dice...* um, how do you say, I had hoped for it to be the climax of the evening."

Allie blushed. She'd already been virtually on the verge of a climax hours earlier when they danced. And she'd brought that to an abrupt and screeching halt.

"I'll have to hand it to you—this is the best climax I've had in ages." She blanched the minute the words came out of her mouth.

"Cara," Francesco said, placing his hand over Allie's as they sat side by side, their gazes skyward. "Then perhaps you haven't been looking in the right places." He let out a quiet, throaty laugh.

The sky filled with brilliant colors in the shapes of chrysanthemums, hearts, and starbursts. Allie looked around, and the few couples that had been on the lawn near them were now no longer focused on the fireworks but instead were sprawled out and deeply engrossed in make-out sessions. She had to admit to a tinge of envy.

But Francesco leaned over, his mouth close to hers, and he reached out and caressed her breast, ever so softly. Despite herself and her willpower, Allie let out a moan. Which she figured gave him permission to advance the troops. Because before she knew it, his lips were on her lips, his tongue probing hers, exploring her mouth, and he'd eased her flat onto the ground as their kiss deepened and fireworks exploded above them.

"Cara, I've been desperate to do this all night long," Francesco said, leaning over her as one hand quickly slid beneath her top—his top, really—and found her naked breast, her nipple hard and waiting for his touch. *"Ti voglio scopare tutta la notte."* I want to fuck you all night long.

Okay, Allie didn't have a clue what he'd murmured in her ear, but the way he said it indicated he was only vocalizing what she was thinking. Somehow it broke down her resistance. She reached over to his chest and gently stroked her hand along his body, petting him as if he were her very own bunny. She furrowed her fingers into the hair on his chest, then traced the outline of his nipples before inching her hand lower along his torso, feeling the rigid outline of his solid abdomen.

He moaned… and lowered his head to her breast, bathing her nipple with his warm, wet tongue and drawing it into his mouth and sucking. It was Allie's turn to moan, and she turned to see if anyone nearby had noticed, but by then everyone else was too far gone in their own little passionate goings-on to pay one whit of attention to what they had going on.

Allie lay sprawled on the grass as brilliant colors exploded across the sky. Her Italian lover suckled her breast while his thigh slid up between her legs and pressed against her center, which forced her to rub herself against him because, well, because she could. She gyrated her pelvis against him, needing more.

Never in Allie's life had anything felt so good and so right as at this very moment, beneath the umbrella of a rainbow of exploding colors, the warm night air and the warmer feel of his skin and his mouth on her body. She combed her fingers through Francesco's thick hair as his hand slipped lower to undo the button on her white shorts, then quickly slid the zipper down. He eased his fingers beneath the edge of her panties and groaned loudly when he made contact with the slick lips of her pussy and her swollen clitoris.

"*Carissima*," he said on a growl.

He went promptly to work, methodically circling his fingers along her center, spreading her juices to ease the path. Which didn't require much effort since she was already practically soaking through her panties. All the while his tongue, teeth, and lips played with her tits. Allie thrust her hips toward his fingers, encouraging him onward, and soon he pressed a finger deep inside of her, curling it toward her pelvis to reach that perfect place.

Allie could barely think, she was so caught up in the sensation of this man working his very talented wiles on her body, stroking and sucking and biting till he had her on the brink.

"Francesco," she pleaded, panting, her body moving of its own volition, pressing toward him with a near-desperate sense of urgency. "I need to feel you inside of me."

Francesco pressed another finger into her slick center, then added a third, mimicking what she was talking about. "Cara, you want my cock to fill up your tight *figa?*"

"*Si,*" Allie said, feeling like Italian was the way to go, and this was one of the few words she wasn't embarrassed to say. "*Si, si, si.*" Yes. Now. *I want your cock in me now.*

"Prontissimo."

It seemed like forever till he granted her wish, but somehow he managed to pull a condom from his wallet while she unzipped his pants, shifted his briefs, and pulled his rather magnificent cock out.

"Ah, Francesco, *perfetto,*" she purred, reaching for the condom to slide it over the head of his cock and down the solid length. She'd heard the word many times since arriving in Italy. Perfect. And his cock was absolutely perfect, and she would go mad if he didn't put it where she needed it now.

"*Cara, apri le gambe.*" Spread your legs.

In quick succession, he shoved her shorts off, spread her legs with his knees, and thrust his cock deep inside her. They both moaned as he held himself still for a moment and she adjusted to his girth.

He leaned in and whispered into her ear. "*La tua figa è così umida.*" Your pussy is so wet. He tortured her by slowly withdrawing himself from her, finally holding only the head of his cock at her entrance.

"More," she said with a sigh, pressing her hips toward him.

He leaned into her ear. "*Strofinati la clitoride,*" he said. "Rub your clit for me. *Venite sul mio cazzo.* Come on my cock, cara."

Allie had never experienced dirty talk during sex, but she found that it turned her on even more than she'd imagined. She loved that he purred in her ear as he licked it, she loved that he gyrated his cock when he was buried balls deep, and she loved that he was such a talkative, affectionate lover. She reached down to rub herself as he thrust into her again and he groaned.

"*Cara, mi fai eccitare,*" he said, his voice a low rumble in her ear. "You turn me on."

He picked up his pace, thrusting harder and faster. Allie could feel herself getting closer, and she was lost in the sensation of his cock sliding deep inside her, his balls pressed up against her. Then he leaned forward and caught her nipple in his mouth, nipping hard, sending shooting sensations throughout her body, as the fireworks in the sky held nothing to the ones exploding inside her. Allie pressed Francesco's mouth to her breast and shouted his name as her pussy spasmed around his cock. Francesco pumped himself into her faster and on the third thrust, he tensed and stilled, his body shuddering as he came hard inside her.

They lay in silence, breathing heavily for a few minutes, the concussive sound of fireworks erupting every twenty seconds as the finale unfolded above them.

Francesco traced his tongue along Allie's lips and pressed his lips to hers, their tongues mating as their bodies had.

She finally emerged from the fog of the best orgasm she'd likely ever experienced, her eyes darting to one side then the other, to see if anyone near them had witnessed

what they'd done.

"What's wrong, carissima?" Francesco planted kisses along her chin, then her neck, then moved down her body to her breast as he again pulled her nipple into his mouth.

"We just had sex in front of complete strangers, out in the open, for everyone to see." Allie could feel the remorse kicking in. "It's like you've turned me into some kind of exhibitionist."

His chest pressed against her belly and rumbled with laughter, and dammit, it felt perfect. How the hell was she going to extricate herself from this?

Chapter Thirteen

AT Allie's insistence, they lay wrapped in their spare tablecloth-makeshift blanket, her embarrassment at being splayed naked in front of strangers evident. Although everyone around them had been in the same state of undress, Francesco could sense his little kitten was turning cold, both literally and figuratively.

"Come, cara," he said. "Let's get you warmed up a bit."

He tugged up his pants and zipped them, then shifted Allie's shorts up and over her bottom so she could zipper them.

"What if these people recognize me?" she said, clearly still dwelling on her sense of indiscretion. Which to him was crazy—nothing hotter than having sex out in the open. Who cared if someone else was watching? If anything, that made it even more of a turn-on. He hoped that deep down Allie felt the same way—he could think of all sorts of ways to channel that little kinky exhibitionist desire.

"If they do, then they'll likely be impressed and give you a high five for your performance," he said with a laugh as he put their picnic supplies back in the bag. Standing, he held out his hand to help Allie up.

"Stop," she said, giving him a playful shove. "I'm

serious. I've never done anything like this before. It's embarrassing."

Francesco pulled her toward him and pressed his forehead to hers. "*Tesoro mio*. That was the sexiest thing imaginable," he said. "I can't even tell you what a turn-on that was to get naked with you, out in the open, beneath the canopy of exploding fireworks. And to know people nearby were doing the same thing, maybe even watching us, listening to us, *molto sexy*." He shook his hand as if he'd touched something hot.

"Really? You think so?"

"*Certo*," he said. Of course. "*Baciami*." Kiss me. He reached for her mouth, and angling his head, his lips settled over hers, their tongues dancing together. "But now let's get you warmed up."

They clasped hands and Francesco led the way into the building, where they found an elevator. They stepped inside and he pressed the top floor, then inserted a key near the button and turned it. The elevator arrived at the top floor and opened onto a large penthouse apartment with a wall of windows overlooking the river, the reflected lights of the Ponte Vecchio twinkling in the lapping waters below.

"Um, how exactly do you have access to this place?" Allie said as she entered the elegant apartment decorated in grays, whites, and blacks.

"Remember I told you I keep an apartment in Firenze? Well," he said, spreading his arms wide, "this is it."

Her eyes opened wide. "I'm sorry. In my world, 'I keep an apartment in the city' usually means a tiny efficiency overlooking a rat-infested alleyway or a giant rooftop air-conditioning unit."

He shrugged. "What can I say? It's my little pied-àterre for when I have business in Florence or want to get away for a couple of days."

"It's fantastic."

"Let me give you the grand tour," he said, reaching for her elbow to steer her into the apartment.

Along one wall of windows was a balcony, with glassed railings for an unobstructed view. The main room of the apartment had dove-gray walls and a black ceiling, with blond hardwood floors covered with gunmetal-gray area rugs. The living room sported a long, white sofa with extra pillows; a large glass coffee table; and two contemporary gray chairs. The kitchen counters were a dark gray granite embedded with white that looked like frost on a windshield, and the island had a leathered granite surface with black cabinets at its base. Two saucer-shaped pendant lights highlighted the sleek chrome cooktop.

"This is a kitchen meant for cooking," Allie said as she ran her fingers along the muted surface of the island. "But something tells me it's never been touched."

"Maybe it's been waiting for the right person to make use of it," he said, lifting his eyebrow.

"I could do some serious damage in this kitchen," she said. "And by damage, I mean that in the best of ways."

"Ah, so you're a cook?"

"I love to cook. But haven't lived anywhere with a kitchen like this, so my life hasn't lent itself to anything all that fancy."

"Then consider this place at your disposal, anytime. Besides," he said, walking down a hallway and curling his finger to encourage her to follow, "if you like the kitchen, I have a feeling you're going to love the rest of the place even more."

They entered a bedroom with a king-sized bed with a gray upholstered leather headboard and crisp, white bedding piled high with pillows. Francesco motioned again for Allie to follow him through a door that opened into a spacious bathroom with a wall of windows overlooking the river and an oversized claw-footed tub.

"I know you needed to warm up a bit, and I can't think of a better way to get warm than in this," he said with a grin as he turned on the faucet to fill the tub.

"You think so, do you?" She walked toward the windows and looked out at the scene below. "Oh, God. I hadn't thought about this. Here I was worried about the people down on the lawn by the river watching us, and I never considered how many people up here could have also seen us." She covered her face with her hands.

"It's tantalizing to imagine, isn't it cara?" He came up from behind and nuzzled her neck as his hands found their way down her body. Quickly he unbuttoned her waistband and rolled down her shorts. His hands slipped down to find her already wet.

"*Carissima, andiamo,*" he said. Let's go.

He shrugged out of his clothes in record time and tugged down her shorts, then lifted her T-shirt over her head. He stood behind her and stared at her naked body in front of the mirrored wall behind the tandem sink. His hands grazed her sides, moving up to cup her full breasts; then his fingers found her nipples and he plucked at them as he pressed himself against her soft skin. Perhaps he'd died and gone to heaven. Their eyes locked in the mirror and she reached behind her to pull him closer, then raised her mouth to his, her tongue reaching for his. He closed his eyes and groaned as he toyed with her nipples. God he couldn't get enough of this woman.

He wrapped his arm around her waist and guided her to the tub, stepping in first and settling down at one end, then coaxing her to join him, where she sat, facing him, in his lap.

"*Tesoro mio.*" He closed his eyes as her hands grasped his cock and began to slide up and down on it. "*È così cazzo incredibile.*" So fucking amazing. "*Ho bisogno di te.*" I need you.

It was as if Allie knew what he was saying as she got on her knees, straddling him, and settled herself down on his hard cock. When he was buried inside her, she gyrated her pelvis and lifted and lowered herself down on him as they both moaned. He caught a nipple in his mouth and she pressed herself toward him, rubbing her clit against him with each stroke his cock made inside her. Her body trembled, her breath coming hard, her moans growing louder until she broke, her body quivering, and he could feel the muscles of her pussy clenching against his cock. That's all it took for him to feel his balls tighten, stars bursting behind his closed eyelids as he exploded into her warm, wet center.

It was official: he was seriously addicted to Allie Ledbetter. Now to figure out how to keep her from slipping away as he knew she would. That would be the challenge to end all challenges. Good thing Francesco had a bit of competitive spirit in him and liked to win.

Chapter Fourteen

ALLIE woke to sunlight streaming through the bedroom window they hadn't bothered to cover last night. That was after, oh, the third or fourth time they'd made love over the course of the night, when they finally made it to the bed itself. There were a surprising number of creative locations in a penthouse to have sex. It turned out perhaps Allie was indeed getting in touch with her inner exhibitionist because it was her idea for Francesco to take her from behind while she leaned over the balcony. With the glass railings.

True, it was late, and more than likely most people were fast asleep. But at some point—probably when his amazing cock was deep inside her and she was susceptible to persuasion and sweet talk—Francesco had convinced her that in Italy, sex wasn't something to be ashamed of, as too often seemed to be the case back home in the land of the Puritans. Allie had found it freeing to simply stop caring about whether someone saw them. She'd imagined it was the same sensation Lola felt when she took flight—free to take off.

Lola. *Crap.* Lola. She needed to get back. The poor thing would be starving. Plus she'd planned to take her through her rounds first thing in the morning.

She got out of bed and found her clothes still on the

bathroom floor and shimmied into her shorts and pulled the T-shirt over her. Ugh, the T-shirt that sported dried blood and dirt from hugging that calciente yesterday. She looked in the mirror to see if there was anything she could do to dust it off, only to realize that you could easily see through the thin white fabric, and her nipples were virtually on display. Oh, God. All evening she'd traipsed about Florence showing everyone her tits. She was so going to kill Francesco.

She went into the bedroom and grabbed a pillow and hit him over the head with it.

"You lied to me," she said with a thud of the pillow.

Francesco opened his bleary eyes, looked up, then smiled. "*Ciao, bellissima. Buon giorno.*" Hello, beautiful. Good morning.

"Don't buon giorno me," she said. "You told me this shirt looked fine on me yesterday, but you can see my breasts through this white fabric. I paraded around Florence like this!"

He grinned. "I know. And they look spectacular."

"But you said the shirt looked fine yesterday."

"And it looks fine today. It looks more than fine. It makes me want to suck on your nipples in the worst way. Come here." He crooked his finger, an impish grin on his face.

"But what about you saying it was fine?"

"Cara, it was fine. You didn't ask me if it was at all see-through. You asked me if it looked fine. And I stand by my word. Besides"—he sat up and tugged on her arm, trying to get her to return to bed—"imagine how many men got hard watching you walk by. And how many women were jealous of those gorgeous tits of yours."

She shifted her eyes one way, then the other. "Well, you do have a point there." She always did like her breasts—they were definitely one of her better features.

"Then what are you doing dressed?" he pulled her into bed so that they were spooning. He wrapped his arms around her, pressed his body up against her back, then began to nuzzle her neck.

"Francesco, I need to get back. I forgot about Lola."

"Lola?" he said.

Then she remembered he wasn't to know about Lola. "Never mind. That's a silly word my friend and I used to use when we had a lot of work to do."

"Lola?" He pressed his cock against her behind, and for a second, Allie wanted to forget all about Lola and get lost with this man and his very skillful body.

"Seriously, I have something I have to do that I forgot about. As much as I'd love to play more, we need to leave."

Francesco sighed. "Fine. Do I have time to shower?"

"I'm sorry, but no."

"What about a bath?" his eyes twinkled as he said it.

"Decidedly not."

"But, cara, *speravo che avresti succhiato il mio cazzo,*" he said. "I was hoping you would suck my cock. Like you did last night."

"I'll have to give you a rain check on that," she said with a sigh. "But only if you promise to *mangia la mia figa.*"

He blurted out a laugh. At some point in the middle of the night, he'd told her that meant "eat my pussy."

"You're a quick learner."

"I have the best teacher." She reached her arm out to pull him out of bed. "Now, *andiamo.*" Let's go. Allie had learned all sorts of useful things under the tutelage of the sexiest man she'd ever been with. But now, Lola called.

"Wait a minute," Francesco said when Allie told him where she was staying. "You're staying at Giovanetti Vineyards? What are you doing there?"

"Um, through some friends of friends. I heard they had a guest cottage, and someone said I could stay there for a while."

"Huh. I didn't know they rented it out."

"I think it's sort of a gentleman's agreement." *Gentleman's agreement? What the fuck is that supposed to mean, Allie, you dingdong?* "I only mean that I offered to pay, but they turned it down.

"Not a bad place to get to stay for free, though you'd enjoy much better wine at our vineyard." His mouth lifted into a broad smile.

"Well, I suppose beggars can't be choosers."

"Cara," Francesco said, placing his warm hand on Allie's lap, stroking his palm along her thighs, "I would love to hear you beg for my cock, *per favore.*" Please.

She threw him a sly glance. "It wasn't enough for me to beg you last night?"

He shook his head. "I want you to need me so much that you'll beg again and again."

"If you're not careful you might get your wish." Or if I'm not careful, I'll end up with a pile of heartache and a fierce sense of regret.

Francesco pulled up the long cypress-lined driveway of Giovanetti Vineyards, and Allie directed him to a small road that split off and took them to the private guest cottage she was staying in.

He leaned over to kiss her affectionately on the nose. "I had a most exceptional evening, Allie Ledbetter."

She smiled, feeling genuinely good about all that had unfolded in the past day, even if he did dupe her about how see-through the T-shirt was. "You know, you're not such bad company yourself, Francesco Romeo."

"Not bad company? Can we maybe generate a response that's a little less tepid? Or am I going to have to persuade you further?" He dipped his head down and settled his lips on hers, his tongue probing for hers as his fingers inched up beneath her shorts.

"I promise you I'd like nothing more than to continue this inside, so that you can prove to me you are indeed most excellent company—even though to be honest I already knew that—but I have commitments to fulfill."

Francesco slipped his fingers up past the elastic band of her panties and swiped them through her already damp pussy.

He pulled them out and placed his fingers in her mouth, where they both licked them clean. He moaned.

"Cara, I have to be away for about a week, but I want to see you as soon as I'm back." He ran his fingers through her hair, pulling her head closer as they kissed. "But we can talk by phone, and maybe we can get creative."

Allie frowned. Just her luck the man she suddenly starts falling for is pulling a runner, dammit.

"Hand me your phone," she said, and she entered her phone number into his contacts list, then sent herself a text, so she knew it worked. "Now you have no excuse to say you lost my number. I look forward to getting creative with you."

"*Grazie mille, il mio micio.*" Many thanks, my little pussycat.

Finally Allie extricated herself from the kiss and waved her fingers as she backed away from the car, mounted the steps to the cottage, and opened the door. As much as the idea of being without Francesco sounded downright torturous, given the circumstances, she had a sneaking suspicion that his absence was the best thing for her anyhow. And she was sure her good friend Harper would thoroughly agree.

Chapter Fifteen

ALLIE worked with Lola throughout the day, taking a little break to apologize to Giovanni in person for her disappearance. She'd texted him at the time, but still needed to say something.

"So, what did you end up doing?" he asked.

"I met up with some friends by pure accident," she said, feeling awful for the lie, but she suspected he would not be keen on her fraternizing more with Francesco. She didn't want to chance his telling her to steer clear altogether. That would be super awkward because she didn't want to avoid him. They'd had far too much fun together.

"I didn't know you knew anyone in Toscano," he said as he watched Lola diving from high.

"I'd heard from an old sorority sister of mine that some other sisters were in Florence, so it worked out great."

"Where did you stay?"

"Oh, um, they were at a hostel and I ended up sharing a bed with one of them."

"I hope you had a fun time. I wish I had warned you not to travel into white territory while dressed in Azzurri colors."

Allie blushed. "It worked out fine," she said, averting his gaze. "I bought a white shirt on the street and changed into that. All good." Lola landed on Allie's shoulder, and she fed her one last piece of raw quail meat, flailing it a bit to distract Giovanni from the conversation.

"Well, I'm beat," she said. "Think I'll go to bed early tonight. Thanks again for taking me to the Calcio. It was quite an experience!"

Once back in her cottage, she picked up the phone and called Harper.

"Ciao!" her friend said when she picked up the phone.

Allie laughed. "You picking up Italian while I'm gone?"

"I quit after the first word. But I hope for your sake you're learning plenty."

If only she knew how much she was learning.

"Yeah, I learned how to ask a guy to eat my pussy in Italian."

Harper sputtered into the phone. "Oh, my God. That would be hilarious. I can practically see you with some random guy throwing that line at him."

Allie uncorked the wine she'd opened the other day and poured a glass. "What if it wasn't some random guy?"

"Wait. You mean you're not kidding me? And who wouldn't be a random guy there? Please don't tell me you did your boss because that would be a huge mistake."

"Of course not. Besides, he has a girlfriend. Who is very beautiful but I can't speak to her because she doesn't speak English."

"I don't care about his girlfriend. I want to know a) how do you ask someone to eat you out in Italian and b) who did you ask this of?"

"Repeat after me: *mangia la mia figa*," Allie said, giggling.

"You'd better hope they don't have recording devices in your cottage."

"It's Italy, Jen. They'd probably pay me more if they knew I was tossing out sexual demands like rose petals at a wedding processional."

"You are dragging your feet getting to the nitty gritty, All. I need the who."

"I'm worried you're going to be mad at me for this."

"I'm so uninformed about your life in Tuscany that I can't imagine I could be mad at you. I mean how bad could it be? You have a bird you fly around all day long, you hardly know a soul. You have dinner, you drink some wine, you go to bed. Rinse, lather, repeat. It can't be that bad."

"I don't think it's bad at all. In fact it's quite good. Make that better than good."

"And the big reveal is…"

"Francesco Romeo—"

"You told him to eat your pussy?"

"Right?"

"Was this out of the blue or was there some appropriate context?"

"Um, it was after we'd done it on a riverbank beneath a canopy of fireworks, and in a claw-footed bathtub in his penthouse apartment overlooking the Arno River, and then on his balcony—"

"You didn't even know how to find the guy and the next thing I know you're having wild sex with him? What happened in between?"

"I went to this big, crazy event in Florence with my boss and his girlfriend. Who ends up in the empty seat next to me but Francesco Romeo. We talked during the thing—but only because the girlfriend was seated next to me on the other side and as I said, it wasn't a great conversation starter when we didn't have a common language between us—"

"Thank God you didn't ask *her* to eat your pussy."

"That was before I learned how to say it."

"Nevertheless, continue."

"Well, this big crazy, weird sporting-event-slash-cage-match ends, and the crowd is going absolutely nuts. It's off-the-rails insane, and next thing I know, I've lost Giovanni and there is Francesco, offering to be my protector, and then showing me an incredibly good time in Florence."

"I'll say you had a good time. Did you reciprocate?"

"Stop! Yes. I mean, well, sure. But he took me all over the city and we had a fantastic time and he surprised me and there were fireworks and oh, God, Jen, it was different from anything I've ever done in my life."

"So now what? You learn more Italian porn phrases that you then put to good use?"

"I can only hope." Allie took a sip of water. "But seriously, before I had vowed to avoid him but now I want nothing more than to be with him."

"Does that mean you're waiting by your phone for him to call you?"

Allie sighed. "Sort of, but not for the reason you think.

See, he told me he's going away for a week. We're supposed to get together when he's back."

"How do you know he's not using that as an excuse because he's got to spend the next several days with his fiancée planning their wedding?"

"Fiancée? Are you serious? You are being such a Debbie Downer! I had this fantastic time with this lovely man, and now you're determined to convince me he's two-timing me?"

"I'm only saying, proceed with caution. I'm glad you're having fun and even happier that you got him to mangia your figa or whatever that is. That's always a good sign when a guy'll do that."

"So are you saying I should forge on and see how things go? Or should I retreat and cower in a corner in case he's going to dump me?"

"Without question, you need to keep with the figa mangia-ing. Hope for the best and proceed with a hint of caution in case there's a fiancée lurking. Deal?"

"Deal."

"On the condition that you keep me apprised of this new vocabulary you're learning because I think I could probably influence some impressionable young man with Italian dirty talk.

"I'm on it. Ciao, ciao, *mia amica*."

"Arrivederci, Allie."

Allie took a sip of her wine and curled up on the sofa, her phone opened to her Google translate app, trying to come up with some additional linguistic challenges for her Romeo.

Chapter Sixteen

ALLIE spent much of the day out in the vineyard, working for hours with Lola in the hot summer heat. As much as she loved working with Lola, sometimes she wished there was someone she could trade off with, if only to get more of a break. Once the starlings showed up en masse, it was going to get even more exhausting. In the past, she'd partnered with other falconers, but to make the trip across the ocean for this job, she wanted to be sure it made sense before enlisting the help and taking on that added expense and responsibility. But she was starting to think she'd made a computational error: this property was large enough that she could easily use another raptor to help manage the demand.

It was probably too late for this year's harvest, but it was something she would need to contemplate if she was invited back next year.

She'd gone to market in the village of Santa Romeo that morning and picked up ingredients to prepare a fresh caprese salad with gorgeous heirloom tomatoes, fresh basil, and homemade mozzarella made by a little old nonna who'd clasped Allie's hands in hers while promising her she'd love it. She purchased some cheese ravioli (made by another little old nonna, naturally) and made a simple red sauce by cooking down some tomatoes with a bit of onion, salt, and butter.

Right when she finished cleaning up after her meal, her phone rang. She didn't recognize the local number.

"*Carissima.*" Her heart skipped a beat when she heard the voice. It was Francesco. She'd forgotten to enter his name in her contact list when she sent that text from his phone. Good thing she answered it.

"Francesco?"

"I've missed you, Allie Ledbetter," he said. "Tell me what you've been doing while I've been away?"

Unfortunately she couldn't share much of what she was doing with him, which was starting to feel awfully dishonest. But she could tell him about her other experiences.

"I spent a few hours poolside over the past few days," she said. "During the hottest time of the day, it's the only thing you can do to keep cool."

"I wish I could be there with you."

"Me too," she said. "I made a sort of Italian meal tonight. I'm not sure if a local boy would be that impressed with it, but I enjoyed it."

"When I get back we'll cook together in my apartment in Florence. Perhaps we could even get creative with some food. Perhaps I could find some alternate uses for tiramisu."

Allie closed her eyes, trying to imagine what he had in mind.

"Such as?"

"Cara, I would begin by sharing tastes of it from my tongue to yours," he said, his voice low and rumbly. "Then I would strip you naked and spoon it on those gorgeous tits of yours and lick it all off."

"Is that all?" Her breath hitched as she spoke.

"Of course not, cara. Next I would spread it on your pussy, and slowly, deliberately, I would lick you clean until you were mad with pleasure."

"I like it when you talk dirty to me, Francesco. Especially in Italian."

"Cara, *mi ecciti molto*. You excite me a lot. *Non posso smettere di pensare a te*. I can't stop thinking about you. You and that *stretto poco figa*, that tight little pussy of yours. Now it's your turn, cara."

"I've been spending some time on Google translate, Francesco. Please forgive me if I get this wrong. *Voglio succhiare il tuo cazzo*."

Francesco groaned. "You're killing me, cara mia. You want to suck my cock?"

"Si. E voglio che leccate la mia figa."

"Cara, your Italiano is *eccellente*. Excellent. But even better than your words are your desires. My tongue yearns to slowly trail along your wet pussy, to lap up your juices after I've driven you mad with pleasure. And my cock is desperate to slip into the warm, tight heat of that beautiful *figa* of yours, but only after I've teased you by sliding it along your lips and around your clit until you beg me to fill you with my cock."

"Jesus, Francesco. I wish you were here right now to honor your commitments. Now I'm desperately horny with no one to service me." She laughed.

"*È per questo che hai le dita*. That's why you have your fingers."

"Right here? Now? With you, on the phone?"

"Better yet, we could FaceTime. The next best thing to

being with you. Hang up. I'm calling you back in a second."

Allie blanched. Could she do *that*? With him watching? On his phone? It seemed like it would look weird and awkward. But damn, he had her so hot and bothered, she was game for giving it a go.

Her phone rang and it was Francesco, on FaceTime.

"Cara, first I want you to take off your clothes for me."

"You first," she said, still a bit apprehensive about it.

"No problem," he said, quickly stripping off his button-down shirt and peeling off his pants. He kept on a pair of black bikini briefs that barely contained his burgeoning erection. "Now you, Allie."

She lifted her camisole top and pulled off her running shorts, which left her with a tiny pair of lavender lace panties. "Now what?"

"Ahh, carissima, I love to look at you. So beautiful. I want you to play with your nipples while I watch."

First she grazed her hands over her breasts, slowly, for emphasis, then licked her fingertips one by one, then pinched her nipples between wet fingers, squeezing and pinching them.

"How does that feel?"

"Good, but it feels better if it's you doing it."

"I know, but until then… Now I want you to slide your hand down your belly, slipping your fingers beneath your panties." Allie complied. "What does it feel like?"

"Wet. And hot." She moaned. "Francesco, I want you to play with your cock while I do this."

"I'm one step ahead of you, cara." She looked and saw that he'd slipped his cock from his briefs and was already twisting his hand up and down his length. "But I want you to get closer. I want to watch you come. Can you insert your fingers into your pussy for me? But don't touch your clit yet."

She did as he asked and moaned again. "What now?"

"Does that feel as good as it does when my cock is filling you up?"

"It's so much more when it's your cock in me."

"Allie, pull down your panties. *Voglio vedere la tua figa bagnata.* I want to see your wet pussy." Allie did as he asked. "*Apri le gambe.* Spread your legs."

She watched him work his hand faster on his cock. The head was swollen and he used the precum to lubricate himself.

"If you were here I would sit on your cock and ride you hard like a wild horse."

"*Mamma mia*, Allie, you're making me crazy." His breathing was hard and his eyes closed briefly. "I want you to lick your wet fingers, cara. Slowly. Pretend it's my mouth savoring every drop of your juices."

Allie was so turned on she squirmed, trying to close her legs to provide friction on her clit as she licked her fingers, staring into his eyes on the screen of her phone, excited knowing how much it excited him to watch her.

"Carissima, I wish I was with you right now. I'm close to coming. Are you?" She nodded. "Now I want you to play with your clit. Rub your fingers along your lips and around your clit. I want to watch you make yourself come."

At last, she was able to work her fingers along her clit, her juices so profuse her fingers slid easily. She felt the buildup deep inside her pelvis, the tingling that traveled all the way to her nipples.

"*Sto venendo.* I'm coming. Come with me, cara." Allie

looked on the screen to see Francesco lost in pleasure as he stroked his penis. She could feel her orgasm closing in on her as she made figure eights around her clit and her lips, faster and faster until she heard Francesco shout out her name as he exploded onto his hand, his cum spurting in waves onto his belly as he twitched and milked himself dry. That was all it took for Allie to go over the top as she squeezed her eyes against the bright lights bursting behind her eyelids, the waves of spasms echoing through her pelvis for what seemed minutes.

As her breathing returned to normal, she opened her eyes to see him smiling at her.

"That was *perfetto*, Allie Ledbetter. The only thing better would have been to be there in person."

"Wow," she said, her breathing finally slowing down. "I've never done that before."

"You've never pleasured yourself before?"

She laughed. "To the contrary. I've gone on long dry spells between men. I'd be crazy not to. But I've never done that in quite the same way."

"Almost makes you look forward to time apart."

"Not quite," Allie said. "Hurry back so we can try out that tiramisu idea of yours."

She fell asleep that night thinking of other creative food play ideas and determined she was going to have to figure out how to make some homemade brownie batter to contribute to the cause.

Chapter Seventeen

GIOVANNI wasn't kidding. When the starlings showed up, they hardly had to announce themselves, there were so many thousands of them: *uno stormo di storni*. A flock of starlings. Understatement of the year. More like a tsunami of them.

They were terribly destructive birds that could wipe out a fruit crop with little effort. She knew of vintners in California that lost 90 percent of their yield thanks to the destruction of such birds. And while covering the vines with netting could help to mitigate the problem, nets were expensive and cumbersome and required a lot of people doing manual labor to cover the crop adequately.

Allie was out in the grape fields with Giovanni, who talked about what a hassle pest control was for grape growers.

"Wild boar are the worst. But we have plenty of nuisance creatures to contend with, including porcupines, deer, foxes, hare, rabbits, and mice. We plant certain ground cover crops that encourage both good insects, like ladybugs, and good birds to nest low and eat those rodents—that helps.

"But in the sky, we've tried blasting cannons to no avail. Not to mention the neighbors hated that sound.

Scarecrows, no use. Mylar strips to scare the birds—forget it. They learn quickly that they're not a threat. Which is why I hope you are going to be the answer to my prayers. And if so, next year we can bring you back with more falcons and another falconer perhaps."

"I think you'll be pleased with what Lola can do."

Lola was perched on Allie's shoulder as Allie took in the view. After whispering some words of affection into Lola's neck, Allie removed her helmet, stroked her, then sent her skyward, where Lola began to flap her wide wings and make large circles around the vineyard. You could see her four-foot wingspan from far away.

Allie didn't want Lola to hunt while up there; she simply wanted the raptor to let her presence be known. She waved her rope in a circular motion to lure her back. Once Lola returned, Allie secured her helmet over her head to settle her down, then rewarded her with a piece of frozen quail she retrieved from her waist pack. She wanted Lola just hungry enough to hunt, but not hungry enough to want to eat when she was in the air.

"So Lola isn't a killing machine after all?" Giovanni asked.

"Not at all. We don't have time for her to catch and eat an entire bird," Allie said, gently stroking her bird. "I want her up there as though she's the bouncer at a bar. Letting everyone know if they make one wrong move, they're out. And as long as she does that, she'll be rewarded with the raw treats I give her.

"It also helps me to regulate her weight—it matters a great deal what weight they're flying at, as they can get sluggish if too heavy, so I have to make sure she's in top shape and not overfed."

"Who knew there was such a science to falconry?" Giovanni reached out to stroke the back of the bird.

"Birds like starlings are a particularly big problem, as you know, because they form such large flocks. There's safety in numbers. The falcon serves to divide and conquer, pushing those enormous flocks into smaller segments and splitting them up smaller and smaller. This helps to encourage good birds to stick around, rather than being squeezed out by the bully birds.

"Back home, the giant clouds of starlings will basically block out native birds like quails, sparrows, and bluebirds, which eat insects or seeds instead of grapes. Any way we can help lessen the power of these huge flocks, the better."

"How quickly can we see these huge flocks dissipate?"

"Within a day or two," she said. "Falcons can spot starlings from a half mile away. And falcons have been clocked going two hundred miles an hour. As soon as starlings see a bird of prey in the sky, they skedaddle, and those huge black clouds of birds become smaller and smaller and smaller. Lola can chase away ten thousand starlings in under an hour."

He nodded. "Impressive."

"Giovanni," Allie said, finally mustering up the courage, "may I ask why you don't want Francesco Romeo to know why I'm here?"

"Because Francesco does for the Romeo vineyards what I do here: as vineyard managers we have to get rid of the things that are eating our profits. I suspect that all the good Lola will do for us will make things that much harder for them. Those starlings have to go somewhere. I figure the longer they're unaware of my tactics, the better."

Well, crap. Something told Allie this was not going to

work out in her favor after all.

Chapter Eighteen

IT didn't take long for Allie's fears to come to fruition. She was out in the field with Lola two days later when she heard a diesel engine racing up the long driveway, horn a-blaring.

As the truck drew nearer, Allie saw it was Francesco in hot pursuit of her boss.

"Giovanni Giovanetti," she heard him shouting as he got out of his Range Rover at the first row of vines. "Where the hell are you? What the fuck are you doing to me?"

A host of farmhands rushed to see what was going on, and Allie heard a slew of bad-sounding Italian words being fired at Giovanni. "*Che cazzo è?* What the fuck is this? You have someone sending all of your birds my way? This is ethical? *Stronzo.* Asshole."

She saw a lot of hand gestures accompanying the harsh words and she wasn't sure if she should try to hide or come clean. It was a tough choice: she didn't want to continue to lie to Francesco. Although she hadn't quite lied but rather committed a serious act of omission.

She heard more loud shouting and then Francesco got back in the Range Rover and drove directly toward where Allie was calling Lola back with her feather-tailed rope.

He pulled up and stepped out of the vehicle as Lola landed on her shoulder. She reached into her pouch and rewarded the raptor for a fine job.

"*Scusi,*" she heard him say. "*Cosa pensi di star facendo?*" What do you think you're doing?

Allie turned to see Francesco, the man whose face she last saw in the throes of orgasmic pleasure; only his face was now twisted in rage.

"Allie? Cara—what the hell are you doing? Why are you—"

"Francesco," she said, at a loss for words as she reached toward him, but he backed away. "I'm so sorry. I didn't know—"

"You didn't know what? That you were ruining our crops because this *puttana* paid you to do so? When were you going to tell? After everything was destroyed, now that you've sent tens of thousands of birds to eat our grapes?"

Allie covered Lola's head with the hood and stroked her to settle her down. She stood there in her Ranger Rick-wear, looking at her lover, trying to convey with the pain she felt in her eyes that this wasn't intentional.

"You have to believe me—this is all a huge misunderstanding."

"The only misunderstanding is that I thought I was falling in love with you. Instead it was likely all part of Giovanni's scheme to compete against us. He knows Giovanetti wines can never truly compete with Romeo wines on the quality of the product. So instead, he set out to ensure that we didn't have anything left to harvest this year."

"I should have known never to trust you. *Vai*

all'inferno." Go to hell.

He spit on the ground as he climbed back into his Range Rover and drove away, leaving a cloud of dust in his wake and a crestfallen Allie Ledbetter to boot.

Who knew a girl and her bird could cause so much trouble? Here she was, innocently minding her business, hired to fix a problem with the help of her beloved Lola. Not to get in the way of warring winemakers or whatever the hell had happened today. And in the process, the man she knew, who, despite herself, she'd begun to carry a serious torch for, now hated the very ground she walked on.

Allie had cried for at least an hour and was tired of the sobs even though they kept springing from her intermittently.

Eventually she picked up the phone and called Harper.

"It sounds super loud where you are," she said when Harper answered the phone.

"I'm on another stupid date," she said.

"Please tell me this one is better."

"Not by much," she said. "This guy's fiancée dumped him a month before the wedding. He can't seem to get over it."

"Poor guy," Allie said, thinking people had worse problems than she did. "How long ago was that?"

Jen sighed. "I think it was nine years ago."

"Oy," Allie said. "It probably is time for him to move on. Or at least try therapy. Speaking of therapy—I'm in need of some. Can you talk?"

"Hell to the yeah," her friend said. "I put the lid down on the toilet, and I'm parked here for as long as you need me. Pull up a seat and unload your woes. Your friend Jen will make it better."

"I don't think you can this time, Harper. But at least I can cry to someone else rather than to myself."

"You've been crying? Did that player Romeo boy do something to you?"

"I'm afraid it's more like what I did to him."

"It can't have been much because this is you we're talking about. I mean the most you do is drink one too many glasses of wine once in a blue moon. You play with birds for a living, for goodness' sake. How much trouble could you have caused?"

Allie thrust her lip out in a pout. "A lot, if what your bird is doing is leading to the destruction of his entire business."

"Oh, shit," Harper said. "The grapes. His grapes. He's next door. Lola is sending him some unwanted visitors…"

"Yup. Giovanni, the guy who hired me, wanted me to keep quiet about why I was here. I hadn't figured out quite why. But then today when Francesco found out, well, it was ugly."

"How ugly?"

Allie heaved the most soulful of sighs. "He spit on the ground at my feet."

"Oooh. That sounds like one of those Italian curses you hear about. What's that thing called, the malocchio, the stink eye?"

"You mean he cursed me when he spit at my feet?"

Harper backpedaled. "Oh, honey, no, I didn't mean to say that. I meant it sounded like something like that. I think he probably spit there because his mouth was dry from yelling so much. Or something like that."

"You are so full of shit."

"I'm making it up as I go along here. I'm entirely unfamiliar with evil eyes and curses. Not my territory."

"Well, what am I supposed to do? I was falling hard for him. He's so sweet and thoughtful and sexy. We had FaceTime sex, Jen."

"Yikes. Seriously? Weren't you worried that you'd look terrible on a phone screen?"

"Well, yeah, but I guess the whole horniness thing took over and I stopped thinking about that."

"Was it good?"

"Amazing. I highly recommend it. Only not with the guys you've been dating lately."

"You went from FaceTime sex to the malocchio, or at least a loogie on the ground that wasn't intended as a kind gesture."

Allie started to cry again. "Yeah. And I'm sad. I was only doing my job. I didn't mean to hurt him."

"Then tell him that."

"I tried."

"And?"

"That was roughly when that spit came flying at my feet."

"Well, maybe give it a couple of days, then maybe FaceTime him, naked. Guys can't resist that for very long, you know."

Allie sighed. "I guess that's an option. I'll think about

it. Meantime, thanks for being there. It helped to hear a friend's voice. Go back to your bad date. I'll figure things out here."

"Take care, sweetie. It'll work out. I know it will."

Too bad Allie was just as certain it wouldn't.

Chapter Nineteen

FRANCESCO was steaming mad as he drove the ten minutes from Giovanni's vineyard to his. Who the hell did she think she was—was she like a total spy? Did he plant her, first at the party, to lure him into complacency, then at the Calcio Storico? To think that rotten Giovanni conveniently left because he knew that Mr. Nice Guy Francesco would save the day. What a sucker he'd been.

When he arrived at the Romeo estate, he entered through the gardens behind the palazzo, up the grand marble staircase, and into the great hall, then decided to divert to the kitchen. Maybe a good meal would put his mind in a better place while he could contemplate how to handle this situation. Whatever went on between him and Allie was over and done with, but he still had to devise the best way to kill Giovanni, preferably with his bare hands. And how to do away with the dead body. That was important.

But those damned scavenger birds showing up to dine on his grapes instead of Giovanni's? What the fuck? That was such an asshole maneuver; he had to come up with some type of revenge. He wondered if he could find who Allie's frenemy was, some falconing rival he could bring in to out-falcon her. Maybe his falcon could eat her falcon for lunch. That would be perfect. He'd show them both. Meanwhile, the minute Sandro got wind of this, he was going to have his ass on a silver platter. Talk about a worst-case scenario.

As luck would have it, who did he run into but Alessandro.

"I've been looking everywhere for you, Francesco." He knit his brow and pursed his lips tightly.

Francesco held up his hands in surrender. "Not as if I've been hiding from you, so you can't have looked very far."

"Listen, what the fuck is going on with the damned starlings?" He came up right in his brother's face, combative as ever. "All of a sudden, we're being invaded. You had one job, and you've failed at it. I've had everyone outside banging pots and pans, and we've shot off the cannon three times today. And you're fucking nowhere to be found."

"Look, Sandro, calm the fuck down." Francesco glared at him. On a good day, his brother could have the personality of a pesky terrier nipping at your ankles. But when he got angry—particularly at something negatively impacting what he considered to be his vineyard, even though it belonged to the entire family—well look out because he could be his very own Mount Vesuvius erupting.

"Boys, boys!" Their mother, Fabiana, clapped her hands loudly as she strolled into the kitchen in her scuffy slippers and housecoat. Clearly she was taking it easy today. "Stop with the arguing and tell me what's going on." She reached for each of their hands, probably in an attempt to keep them from punching each other.

"Your idiot son here has failed miserably to keep the damned storni at bay. They've shown up in numbers like I've never seen before. This after he reassured me he had everything under control."

"Sandro could you ever shut your mouth and let me talk? I know you love to hear yourself blather, but the rest of us don't care to listen to you bullying us, got it?"

"Can you both calm down and explain to me what happened?" She pointed to two chairs in the kitchen and made them each sit in one. "Now, Francesco, you go first since it's clear you're the aggrieved brother here."

"I had everything in place, Mamma," he said. "We got netting, and I had the cannons at the ready. I have farm hands assigned to make noise. I got the Mylar flags set up. I'd even just returned from a meeting to discuss hiring a falconer from the south of France to chase the storni from our grapevines." He stood and paced. "But when I returned this morning, I found out that miserable piece of shit Giovanni already hired someone to do exactly that and is driving the storni to our property. He gets a twofer that way: he saves his grapes while destroying ours. He's always been covetous of our fame, that our wine is heralded as the best in Chianti. This was a perfect way for him to exact revenge for whatever inadequacies he has for his small dick."

"Francesco! Bite your tongue," his mother said. "I think there's been a grave misunderstanding."

"Oh, no, there's no misunderstanding," Sandro said, piping in. "He does have a small dick. And I've seen the clouds of storni coming from the direction of their vineyard."

"Boys, please, let me speak." Fabiana was short in

stature but tall in presence. With her cropped salt-and-pepper hair and her commanding voice, she could hold those boys in rapt attention even while standing there in her bathrobe. "First off, I hate it when you boys fight. It's like you scream at each other before even figuring out what the deal is. You're grown men. Act like it. Secondly, Elettra Giovanetti and I had talked about this falconer who they were trying out this year. I knew all about it because she and I discussed sharing efforts with this. There was no malicious intent on the part of Giovanni."

Francesco squinted at her. "Wait a minute. You knew about this but didn't tell me?"

"Caro," she said. "I'm so sorry. I meant to, but I suppose I got busy with that charity event I've been working on for the soup kitchen in Florence. I was so caught up in it that I dropped the ball. I'm sorry."

"But Allie, she was keeping secrets from me. She never told me why she was here, and then, and then there she was—"

"This Allie you're talking about. Is she the young woman from the costume party?"

Francesco frowned. "You knew about that?"

"She's the one you got the hard-on over? The blue ball-inducing kitty cat?" Sandro said.

They both held their fingers to their lips and shushed him loudly.

"Please, *mio figlio*. It didn't take a genius to see that you two had stars in your eyes for each other. And then when you dropped everything to be with her after the Calcio—"

"You knew about that?" Jesus, did she have cameras fixed on him everywhere?

"Of course. Your sister told me how you disappeared

despite your plans to watch the fireworks together for the *festa di San Giovanni*."

Francesco breathed a sigh of relief. Thank goodness there weren't cameras on them—that he knew of, at least—when he made love to Allie along the banks of the Arno.

"Can a man have no privacy around here? And you all wonder why I keep a separate apartment in Firenze." He rolled his eyes.

Then it hit him: he'd been the hugest of assholes to Allie. She hadn't done anything wrong and he freaked out on her. She would never understand why he acted that way. What an idiot. Here he finds this woman he's crazy for, and he sabotages the relationship before he can even ensure that she's on board with it. He shook his head and sighed.

"So you see, it's not Giovanni's fault, nor is it your young woman's fault. It's all mine."

"Look, I don't have time to concern myself with my brother's love life," Sandro said, getting up from the chair. "I have a winery to run. I want the fucking birds gone before our crop is annihilated. Figure it out, prontissimo." He dusted off his hands as if he'd been working hard in the fields. Francesco threw him a dirty look as he left.

"Francesco," his mother said, stroking his cheek. "You look so downtrodden. What can I do to help?"

Francesco shook his head. "It's too late, Mamma. I said some unforgivable things to Allie when I went over to the Giovanettis. She'll never talk to me again, let alone have me back."

His mother reached up to scratch his head, an affectionate gesture he'd loved as a child. "Then let's figure out how you can win her back. First of all, you need to apologize. Every woman loves to hear a man admit he was wrong—since so many of you are terrible at doing that. You can be the standard-bearer for men everywhere who never say they're sorry. And while you're at it, why don't you bring a tray of your mamma's tiramisu. No self-respecting woman would turn that down."

Good Lord, was she privy to their private conversations as well? Did she know about the tiramisu fantasy too?

"Now I'll reach out to Elettra and we'll figure out how we're going to work together to keep the storni away. In the meantime, while I make the tiramisu, you go clean yourself up so you're halfway presentable and try to woo your young lady back."

Chapter Twenty

ALLIE stepped into Giovanni's office, nervous about what she was about to say.

"Ciao, Allie," he said, greeting her with the now-familiar two-cheek kiss. "You're doing great work. I apologize for the rudeness of my neighbor, but that's to be expected."

Allie nodded her head and frowned. "Yeah, well, that's what I'm here to talk about, Giovanni." She paced the floor, anxious about having to call her boss out on his intentions. "That was uncool how you put me in the middle of whatever puerile feud or whatever it is you have going on with Francesco. I don't know if you did that on purpose or what, but putting me in silent collusion with you to cause problems for the Romeo vineyard was not right. I'm afraid I'm going to have to tender my resignation. I can't be part of that sort of thing."

Giovanni scrubbed his fingers through his hair, then held his hands up in protest. "Look, Allie, I didn't mean for all that to happen."

"But you did. You made me keep my mouth shut about why I was here, and shame on me for going along with it, but I guess I didn't think you had some underlying intent to cause problems for your neighbors. I thought your mother and theirs were best of friends. Why would you do something like that then?"

Giovanni heaved a sigh. "I didn't exactly intend to do that. But to be honest, it just kind of happened. I guess in some weird way I wanted to pull one over on Francesco. I get so tired of everything being Romeo this, Romeo that, Romeos are the best. And then here I hire you and bring you here from the States, and a damned Romeo falls in love with you?" He held out his hands to reassure her. "Don't get me wrong, I'm very happy with Letitia, and I didn't have designs on you. But it bothered me that it was one more thing that the Romeos were taking over or meddling in. Like one more damned fire hydrant for a Romeo to pee on, when I had the idea first—I was the one who had come up with this great solution."

"One that your mamma had planned to implement in cooperation with the Romeos," a voice said from the doorway. It was Elettra, a tiny woman with a large presence, her arms crossed, her face set in a frown. "Didn't I tell you to talk to Fabiana's sons about working together with the falconer? Wasn't that the conversation we had?" She came over and gave him a bit of a smack across the back of his head, which surprised Allie. She supposed sometimes this was how a strong Italian mamma kept her brood in line. She wasn't terribly disappointed that she'd done it, considering Allie would have loved to have done that herself.

"Allie," his mother said, reaching over to hug her. "Please, cara, let me apologize on behalf of my very rude son for his unacceptably selfish behavior. This is not at all how we Giovanettis operate and is certainly not in keeping with our code of honor. I hope you'll reconsider sticking around while my son makes everything right with the Romeos."

Allie smiled. "Grazie mille, senora Giovanetti." She was proud of the speed-Italian she'd been picking up, thanks to her smutty Google translate efforts. Even in the midst of learning dirty talk in Italian, she had no choice but to learn basic grammar usage. "If it's all the same to you, I'd like to go back to the cottage and think about things for the evening. If I can let you know tomorrow?"

"Certainly, cara."

Elettra gave her son one more dope slap on the way out the door, telling him in no uncertain terms to fix what he broke.

It was getting dark when Allie heard a knock on the door of the cottage. She didn't want to talk to Giovanni anymore. She'd said all she wanted to say, had a raging headache, and was well into her second glass of Chianti while she worked to numb her heartache. To think, this morning she was falling madly for a sexy Romeo and happily out with Lola doing what they both loved to do best, and now, she was likely going to be packing her bird and her bags and heading back home. She couldn't see staying around with the awkwardness of what happened between her and her boss. Plus, with Francesco Romeo so close and yet so far, it was all too much for her.

She stood and shifted the curtain to see who was at the

door, hoping to be discreet but evidently was not discreet enough. As she peeked out the window, there stood Francesco himself, staring right back at her. Weirdly, he was holding a tray of something. Ugh, she did not want to continue the fight from earlier. It was hurtful and unpleasant. Couldn't a girl simply get drunk and drown her sorrows in peace around here?

But she did what a grown-up would do and went ahead and answered the door.

"Francesco." She nodded, frowning.

"Cara—" he started to say, but she held her hand up to stop him.

"Please, Francesco. Don't 'cara' me. I get it. You're pissed at me. You hate me. I fucked up. It's over. So I don't want to rehash anything, and frankly, I want to be left alone."

Francesco reached out for her hand and clasped it in his. "Please, cara, let me speak."

She sighed and shrugged. "Fine," she said. "But I don't want to stand in the doorway while more farmhands watch you rip me a new one. If you're going to scream at me, at least do me the favor of doing it in the privacy of the cottage."

She shut the door, walked across the living room, and sat hunched in the far corner of the sofa. If she could have curled into a fetal position, she would have, but that would have been too weird. She pointed at the other end of the sofa. "I suppose you should have a seat."

He held up the tray he'd been carrying and set it on the coffee table. "First, my mother wanted me to bring you a tray of her homemade tiramisu as an apology for what a complete *asino* her son was to you."

Allie grabbed her phone from the coffee table and typed in something, then held it up for him to see. "Jackass. Of course. Yes, you were a jackass."

He hung his head in shame. "I know. I'm so very sorry. I don't have any great excuses. I angered in haste and I deserve your hatred."

She frowned. "Look, Francesco. I don't 'hate' you. I'm not feeling particularly warm and fuzzy about you, that's for sure after you completely flipped your shit on me."

"I didn't flip my shit. Well, not exactly," he said, knitting his brow. "More like I lost my temper."

"Pot meet kettle. Same difference. Whatever you call it, you were hostile to me. That really upset me."

"I know, cara, and I'm such an idiot for losing my temper like I did. I don't have any excuse for it, but out of nowhere, we were basically under attack and it was coming from here. I went to confront Giovanni only to find out you're the one who's driving the attack against us. How was I supposed to react?"

"Well, a good start would have been to talk to me, rather than accuse me."

He nodded. "You're so right. And I'm so wrong. It's only that, God, I had such intense feelings for you, cara. Like nothing I've ever felt for a woman before. *Sto candendo nell'amore con voi.* I'm falling in love with you, Allie Ledbetter. And to feel this intense and foreign sense of love for someone, only to learn that this person has betrayed you—I know you didn't, but I felt like it—well—"

She held up her hand. "Look, before we get any further, I have something to confess. Because it's not fair for me to make you fall on your sword while I maintain complete innocence."

"I don't understand what you're saying."

"I didn't deliberately deceive you, Francesco. Please understand that. But I am guilty of omitting truths from you, and that in and of itself was deceptive. But I only did it because my boss asked me to not disclose to you why I was here."

Francesco frowned. "So you were in cahoots?"

"Not at all. I was hired by Giovanni, long before you and I met. As with any employment situation, if your boss asks you to keep things under your hat for whatever reason, you do so. I didn't realize that he was intent on causing you harm, though. You have to understand that. I had a relationship with Giovanni before I even knew you. And then, well, things with you and me got out of control so fast. Suddenly my allegiance needed to be toward you, but I didn't know how to handle it with Giovanni. I need to be honest and tell you I behaved in a cowardly way by not coming out and telling you why I was in Chianti."

"But you didn't collaborate with Giovanni to ruin our crop?"

"God, no. I would never do something that malicious. Besides, even if I knew that was his intent—which I didn't—if I learned that it was, I would have stopped immediately and let you know that. I hope you will accept my apology, though I understand it's too late for us." She pointed back and forth between them. "But I'd like to leave it on a good note, so at some point perhaps we might still be friends."

"I could never simply be your friend, Allie," he said.

Tears began to fill the corners of her eyes. "I'm sorry about that, Francesco. I had hoped we could be grown-ups about it and move on."

"I also can't move on," he said, sliding closer to her on the sofa. "Did you not hear what I said to you? I'm falling in love with you. Yes, I want to be best of friends with you, but I want it to be much more than that. Friends, but more importantly, lovers."

Allie squinted at him in confusion. "I'm trying to understand what you're saying. But it's not computing. How did you have this sudden change of heart?"

"Is it lame to say that my mamma made me stop behaving like a fool?" He smiled sheepishly. "When she heard about the birds, she told me that she and Elettra had already discussed some sort of shared effort to eradicate the flocks of storni. But then Mamma forgot to tell me about it—"

"And Elettra expected Giovanni to work with you and your family to get the program off to a start"—Allie shook her head—"but he decided not to."

"I don't understand why." Francesco shrugged. "I always got along fine with Giovanni."

"I think he's jealous of your family's success," she said. "To him, it's as if you've been in a contest with one another. In his mind, he's always tried to compete with the Romeos, only you didn't know about it. I actually don't know if he was deliberate in his actions—rather, maybe it was more that this 'arrangement' triggered some shitty decision-making on his part."

"Yeah, well, I'll be dealing with him—you can be sure of that."

"If it's any consolation, his mother gave him quite the upbraiding."

"Upbraiding?"

She laughed. "Finally a word I can teach you, albeit not

a dirty one." She smiled. "It means to scold."

"So his mother gave him shit?"

"Ohhh, yeah," Allie said. "It is—and has been—her intention all along for the families to work together against a common foe. Unfortunately I got stuck in the middle of things."

"And where does that leave you?"

She sighed. "Well, I tendered my resignation to Giovanni today, after I, too, confronted him for his bad intentions."

Francesco's brows furrowed. "You're leaving, then?"

"I was deciding over several glasses of Chianti exactly what I was going to do," she said, taking a sip of her wine, then holding the glass up higher. "Sorry, it's not Romeo wine."

He held up his hands. "*Nessun problema.*" No worries.

"Would you perhaps consider coming to work for the Romeo family? That is, in conjunction with the Giovanettis? We have a beautiful guest house on our property—much nicer than this little shack." He grinned.

"So Lola and I would move next door?"

He growled as he moved closer to her. "I have a confession to make: as angry as I was, I was super turned on when I saw you in that Boy Scout uniform, your long blond braid draped over one shoulder, that powerful raptor resting on your other shoulder. It was incredibly sexy. Part of me wanted to take you right then and there."

"But you were so angry. How could you want to be intimate with someone you're holding such rage toward?"

"Have you never heard of makeup sex, cara?" He eased himself even closer to Allie until their legs were touching.

"Of course I've heard of it. Not that I've ever been a practitioner of it."

"There's no time like the present, then, is there?"

Chapter Twenty-One

"**CAN** I ask you something?" Allie said as Francesco's hand began to stroke her thigh, and she felt that tingling sensation she'd been missing since he was gone.

"Certainly."

"Did your mother know about that tiramisu thing we talked about?"

He laughed as he leaned over to kiss her. "We can only hope not, but since we've got a whole tray of the stuff, and the two of us couldn't make much of a dent in it as it was intended…"

"Do you think she'd mind, then, if I sucked some of it off your cock?"

Francesco groaned. "Cara, you're killing me."

She leaned over and scooped a serving with two fingers, swiping it onto her tongue.

"Now, remind me what we were going to do with it?"

Francesco's tongue reached out and curled over hers, stealing some of the tiramisu. Then he quickly grabbed her top and pulled it over her head as he stared at her bare breasts. He scooped up tiramisu and smeared it over her nipples, then settled his mouth over first one, then the other, dragging his tongue over the creamy dessert, finally feasting on her nipples.

Allie pushed him away, as she deftly reached for the button of his pants, slipping them off, then scooping more tiramisu, slathering it on his penis.

"*Che un bel cazzo grosso,*" she said, making eye contact with him and grinning. What a nice big cock.

"Cara, your Italian is impeccable," he said as she lapped at his enlarged penis, licking the dessert clean off him before taking him into her mouth and sucking hard. He groaned loudly. "Let me have a turn or this is going to be over before it's begun."

He stripped Allie's yoga pants off and spread her legs, slathering tiramisu on her pussy as he pressed his face to her.

"*Amo quando leccate la mia figa.*" She moaned out loud. I love when you lick my pussy.

He looked up into her eyes. "I'll always take care of my favorite pussy, caro. I promise."

"Meow." She sighed. After all, what more could a girl ask for?

Thank you so much for reading *Big O Romeo!* I hope you enjoyed it! If so, please help others find this book:

1. Help other people find this book by writing a review.

2. Sign up for my new releases email so you can find out about the next book as soon as it's available and get fun giveaways.
http://eepurl.com/baaewn

3. Like my Facebook page.
www.facebook.com/jennygardinerbooks

And I love to hear from readers! Let me know what you think about my books! You can write to me at jenny@jennygardiner.net, and visit me on the web at www.jennygardiner.net.

Keep reading for a sample from **Falling for Mr. Wrong**, the first book in a brand new series.

Falling for Mr. Wrong

Chapter One

IF Harper Landry got stuck with one more blind date who was yet another prime candidate for Loser of the Year, she was afraid she was going to punch the guy. Yeah, yeah, she knew that wasn't a particularly charitable notion. After all, the succession of men she'd agreed to date for a variety of completely idiotic or mercenary reasons clearly couldn't help themselves; they were just pathetic excuses for their species. It wasn't fair to kick someone when they were down, was it? And some of these guys were surely down in the trenches. Then again, surely they could work to amend some of their more obnoxious personality traits.

Like the guy who—before their appetizers had even arrived—started sobbing about his fiancé who'd ditched him. Nine years ago. That was the most depressing date she'd had in ages. Because not only was it a waste of her time—and money, since he insisted they go Dutch—but also he then put her on speed-dial just to bawl to someone he thought gave a care. Because she stupidly expressed empathy for his sorry self. Harper felt all the more foolish because she'd donned false eyelashes for the occasion, optimistically thinking it would brighten up her face. Hell, she could've worn a potato sack and that dude wouldn't have noticed.

Then there was the guy who kept spitting on her face as he badmouthed pretty much every person he spoke about. While drinking himself under the table. She'd never forgive the organist from her mother's church for roping her into that regrettable night on the town with her beloved nephew. Particularly when he vomited at her feet as he got into the taxi she insisted on hailing for him because he was too drunk to drive.

She was really starting to wonder if there was something seriously wrong with her that she simply couldn't discern on her own. Harper didn't want to be vain or anything, but from where she was looking, she was under the impression that she was perfectly fine and normal and pretty and nice. Or at least she presumed as much.

She took a look in the mirror as she readied herself for yet another date with destiny—more like date with desperation—and forced a smile as a sort of spirit-boosting maneuver. She gave herself a couple of reinforcing self affirmations—*I am kind, I am smart, I am friendly, I deserve respect and happiness*—then ran her fingers through her auburn waves, which she thought looked perfectly fine. That certainly couldn't be a deal-breaker with a man. Besides, her hair was really more brown than auburn if she was going to be truthful about it. No guy hated brown hair, did they?

She then practically pressed her face to the mirror, trying to see if she had some particular facial flaws that might turn off a guy. Nope. She had really pretty sea glass-green eyes, sort of cat-shaped, which she always took pride in. She thought it made her look mysterious. But maybe men thought she was too feline, too elusive, because of them? Wait a minute. Because of her eyeballs? That would be so stupid. She wouldn't want to be with a man who was so ocularly judgmental (and was ocularly even a word?).

She tugged on her dress and pressed along it with the palm of her hands where it bunched a little bit along her hips, then turned sideways. Well, damn! She looked pretty amazing, if she did say so herself. She had a perfectly acceptable figure, a beautiful set of legs—and the heels she was wearing only made them look better. So why, oh why, if she wasn't a scaggly, sad-sack loser with bad breath (oh no! was her breath bad?!), was she stuck dating such a rogue's gallery of the lamest men this charming little beach town she loved had to offer?

Could it be her personality? Again, she didn't want to be cocky, but as far as she could tell her friends all thought she was normal. And nice. And funny. Funny was good, right? But did guys think funny was too, like, Seth Rogan, for a girl? Was being funny supposed to be only the domain of raunchy, paunchy comedians? Did guys hate a girl who was a little sarcastic, who loved to crack a good joke? Maybe they didn't like that she sometimes used salty language. After all, she rarely met a good f-bomb she wasn't happy to detonate. Under the appropriate circumstances, of course.

Which would be super hypocritical because any guy would be all over it like white on rice if she talked like that while she was having sex with them. Didn't guys love that? All "fuck me baby," and "Oh, yeah, I fucking love when you do that," and "Oh, your fucking cock is so big," and such. Hmmm, maybe she needed to up the ante in the naked dirty-talk department. But then again, as it was, she wasn't getting anywhere near naked—she wasn't even graduating to the kissing stage—because ugh, given the guys she'd been dating, she'd just as soon never shake the sheets again than compromise her standards by sleeping with those lackluster specimens. She'd settle for her trusty pocket rocket any day over that.

She grabbed her phone and checked the time on it, then ordered up an Uber and went to the curb to wait for it. This way if the date was as horrible as they usually were, she could get stinking drunk and not worry about driving home. All the more important because she was meeting her mystery date—Danny Greevy, a friend of a friend of a friend's friend's uncle's goddaughter, or something like that—at a new restaurant several towns over, so even further from home.

She'd honestly lost track of most of these forgettable men at this point. She almost wondered why she continued to show up for them, hopeless as they always were. She figured she had an optimistic streak that far outpaced her reality, but sometimes hopeful was all you could hang your hat on in this world.

When the driver dropped her off at the designated address, she straightened her dress, wiped a smudge of lipstick off of her teeth she'd noticed when she glanced in the rear-view mirror, and got out of the car. Only to behold her destination: an actual restaurant called Octopussy. Lord help her. The regrettably-named dining establishment featured a mammoth three-dimensional female octopus, whose bulbous body erupted from the top edge of the building like a zit that needed to be popped. Her eight human-style legs (ending in stiletto'd feet, of course) extended around the edges on either side of the establishment as well as down the front wall. Harper was surprised there wasn't an exposed vulva and straggly pubic hair just to make the point about the place. Though no doubt this octopussy would be waxed clean.

She slowly walked the path to the restaurant as if a pirate held a cutlass to her back to force her down the gangplank. To be truthful, she'd probably have been more enthusiastic about that, because at least maybe the pirate would be personable, or—better yet—a little lust-worthy if she was lucky.

Ugh. This place bore all the hallmarks of strip club, which was why she was taken aback when she opened the door and was greeted by a tuxedo-clad maître-d'. *Okay...*

"Um, I think I'm meeting my date here." Harper tucked her hair behind her ear, a nervous habit that gave her something to do while she debated fleeing while the getting was good.

She scanned the restaurant and finally "got" the theme—it was some sort of retro James Bond-esque thing, and the place had all sorts of spy type paraphernalia framed and mounted on the walls. Kind of like how Appleby's might have antlers or old-timey pictures from the heartland or faux tin Pennzoil signs everywhere, only instead it was guns with silencers attached and pictures of James Bond's getaway cars, and an autographed picture of Roger Moore in his heyday. Weird.

"Miss?" The host lifted a questioning eyebrow.

"Landry. Harper Landry. I'm meeting Danny, um—" she pulled out her phone and opened her calendar to find the guy's name again. "Greevy. That's it, Danny Greevy."

Harper heard the door open behind here.

"Danny Greevy at your service," she heard a voice say behind her. She turned to see a man bent at the waist in a bow. He stood up and reached for her hand. "You must be the delightful Harper Landry I've heard so much about.

And you're even more beautiful than I was led to believe."

Harper tried to suppress a grin. This guy actually had potential. First off, he had manners, which was nothing to shrug off. Especially considering one of her recent dates let the door slam on her face when they left a restaurant at the same time. The glass of the door literally hit her in the nose. Needless to say they went opposite directions once outside. Secondly, yowza. He was pretty damned hot. He had sort of dishwater blond hair that seemed to fall into place from its side part as if following orders. He had warm brown eyes, and a dimple in his left cheek.

Wait a minute. She did a mental double-take. Something was awry here. The guy was cute and polite. There must be something wrong with him. Alas, she knew she'd have all evening to discern what his fatal flaw was. And she'd sure as hell figure it out.

Chapter Two

BUT flaws were not jumping out at her. Instead, he kept inching up the "potential" list. Go figure. Add to the list: an unexpectedly charming sense of humor. Turned out Danny had hoped that Harper would get a good laugh out of a restaurant named Octopussy. That was good news on two fronts: one, he had a sense of humor. And two, he obviously delighted in a woman who shared such with him.

"I figure if a date shows up here and storms off, she's not for me," he said as the waiter handed them each a menu. "It's always the easiest way to weed out the stuck-up ones."

"Stuck-up?" Harper said, lifting her eyebrow. "That's not usually the ones I'm contending with. Instead most of my blind dates are developmentally stunted. Like they've spent the better part of the last five years hunkered down in their parents' basement playing video games. They sort of have that pasty-white flesh, they're usually a bit out of shape, and most of the time lacking basic social skills."

Danny shook his head as he ordered a bottle of wine for them both. "I suppose the women I tend to end up on first dates with would be an upgrade to that. But not by much. Mostly they're first and foremost after a ring and a lifetime commitment. Usually by the time dessert is served. They tend to laugh a little too hard at my jokes, fawn over me like a doting grandmother, and treat me like some delicate endangered species—*a single male!*—The dodo bird of this century."

Harper held up her hands in surrender. "Trust me, there will be no pretense of that from me. I'm happy to go on a few dates, but I am decidedly not in search of some elusive Mister Right." She made air quotes when she said that. "After some of the dates I've been fixed up with, I'd be perfectly happy with Mister Have Some Fun." In hindsight, Harper thought perhaps that wasn't the best way to phrase that, but she figured correcting herself would only draw attention to the wayward comment so she let it go.

"Well then, we'll get along just fine." The corners of his mouth turned up and his perfectly straight, white teeth bared for a smile.

He really was such a handsome man.

"You up for some dancing?" Danny said as they chatted over coffee after dinner.

"Where?"

Danny pointed his thumb behind him. "There's a whole other section of this place that's more like a nightclub."

Harper tipped her head in disbelief. "Here? On the poky North Carolina shoreline there's an actual nightclub that I've never heard of?"

"Hard to imagine you're a local and didn't know of it."

"Like I said, the extent of my social life has been going out to the Olive Garden with the godson of Aunt Gertrude or the nephew of Mabel, the church organist, so dancing hasn't been high up on my, uh, dance card." She grinned.

"Then we'd better make up for lost time."

Danny got up and pulled Harper's chair out, then linked arms with her to escort her to the club.

He led her down the hallway, past the doors to the restrooms and the kitchen, where there was an unmarked door. He opened it, ushering Harper through it into what seemed like a large speakeasy, where a jazz band was playing big band music. Danny pressed his hand to her lower back as he led her to the dance floor, where he grabbed her hands and they started dancing.

Harper could still not get over that there was a nightclub a mere twenty minutes or so from her house. She lived in a small beach community, and while there were plenty of things to do nearby, they often entailed the typical cliché beach activities like putt-putt golf, drive-in movies, or all-you-can-eat seafood restaurants. This was downright exciting.

"I love to dance," she said as Danny grabbed her hips and moved along with her. Soon a slow song came on and he pulled her closer. Harper could feel him pressed to her hips and knew he was aroused. Wow. A man. Turned on by her. Downright shocking.

She started to wonder why that was such a stunning turn of events. Was it her lack of confidence that had led her to the drought she'd been in for so long? Of course her thoughts always went down the same path when she started to ruminate on this problem. It all came back to Noah Gunderson. The one who broke her heart when he left her so unexpectedly, just when she thought they were heading toward a lifetime together. If anything chipped away at her self-esteem, that was it. So while she wasn't one to hold a grudge, if there was anyone she'd maybe still consider slugging were she ever to run into him again, it would be Noah.

Thank goodness he left this place years ago. With any luck she'd never see him again.

"Would you like to come back to my place for a nightcap?" Danny whispered into her ear as they slow-danced.

Nightcap? That sounded so pick-up artist-y. It had been a long damned time since Harper had a "nightcap". Or even a daycap for that matter. Daycap. Maybe that would be called "afternoon delight". Crap. She hadn't had that since, well, since that cursed Noah. Three days before he took off for parts unknown, leaving her high and dry and wondering what was so wrong with her that a guy would just up and bail like that after being together for so many years. No wonder she struggled to feel value when it came to men. The man she thought treasured her had discarded her like an old tissue.

Nightcap indeed. It was time to take the bull by the proverbial horns and have herself a fun little nightcap with Danny Greevy.

"A nightcap sounds perfect." She winked at him.

As they walked away from the dance floor, she pulled up the Uber app on her phone and called for a driver, which was there in four short minutes.

It had started to rain while they were in Octopussy,

and Danny offered his suit jacket for Harper to cover her head with as they walked to the curb. Such chivalry. Clearly Danny was a keeper.

When the car pulled up, Danny opened the door and helped Harper into the car. She scooted over to the far side and fastened her seat belt. A few cars drove past as she waited for Danny to get his on, their lights refracting across the raindrops on the car windows.

Danny leaned over and kissed Harper on the nose. "I'm so glad you're coming over to my place. I want you to meet my cat."

Cat? Huh. Sort of an unusual come-on, she thought. Though at least she didn't tell him she wanted him to meet *her* cat! Now that would be a little much.

"Good evening, folks," their driver said as he punched in some data into the GPS on his dashboard-mounted phone. "We'll get you to Cutler Beach in no time."

Harper bristled. That voice. As much as she'd hoped to forget that voice, the minute she heard it, she felt a chill lift the hair on her arms. She'd know that miserable rat-bastard voice anywhere.

"Noah?"

Falling for Mr. Wrong

coming November 14, 2017.

About the Author

Jenny Gardiner is the author of #1 Kindle Bestseller *Slim to None* and the award-winning novel *Sleeping with Ward Cleaver*. Her latest works are the *It's Reigning Men* series, featuring *Something in the Heir, Heir Today Gone Tomorrow, Bad to the Throne; Love is in the Heir, Shame of Thrones; Throne for a Loop; It's Getting Hot in Heir; A Court Gesture;* and her new Royal Romeos series, featuring *Red-Hot Romeo; Black Sheep Romeo, Red Carpet Romeo, Blue Collar Romeo, Silver Spoon Romeo, Blue-Blooded Romeo, Big O Romeo,* and the upcoming *Falling for Mr. Wrong*—the first book in an all new series. She also published the memoir *Winging It: A Memoir of Caring for a Vengeful Parrot Who's Determined to Kill Me,* now re-titled *Bite Me: a Parrot, a Family and a Whole Lot of Flesh Wounds;* the novels *Anywhere but Here; Where the Heart Is;* the essay collection *Naked Man on Main Street,* and *Accidentally on Purpose* and *Compromising Positions* (writing as Erin Delany); and is a contributor to the humorous dog anthology *I'm Not the Biggest Bitch in This Relationship.*

Her work has been found in Ladies Home Journal, the Washington Post, Marie-Claire.com, and on NPR's Day to Day. She was also a columnist for Charlottesville's Daily Progress for over a decade, and is the Volunteer Coordinator for the Virginia Film Festival.

She has worked as a professional photographer, an orthodontic assistant (learning quite readily that she was not cut out for a career in polyester), a waitress (probably her highest-paying job), a TV reporter, a pre-obituary writer, as well as a publicist to a United States Senator (where she first learned to write fiction). She's photographed Prince Charles (and her assistant husband got him to chuckle!), Elizabeth Taylor, and the president of Uganda. She and her family and menagerie of pets now live a less exotic life in Virginia.

Visit Jenny at her website and sign up for her newsletter, her blog, or find her on Facebook and Twitter. And every blue moon she'll post adorable pictures of her pets on Instagram as @thejennygardiner.